MUNICIPAL GOTHIC

13 GHOST STORIES

By

Ray Newman

This collection first published in 2022. All stories, cover image and cover design © Ray Newman.

Foreword © David Southwell, used with permission.

Earlier versions of 'Alice Li is Snowed Under', 'The Curse Follows the Seed', 'Ten Empty Rooms', 'Red Hill' and 'Director's Cut' were previously published on the author's own website. 'Modern Buildings in Wessex' was published as a limited edition booklet in 2020. 'Rainbow Pit' first appeared at horrifiedmagazine.co.uk.

Text set in Plantin MT Pro with headings and titles in Grange

For my brother, Tim, who also saw that strange human shape glowing in the garden of the house next door one Christmas morning many years ago.

Contents

Foreword   7
The Curse Follows the Seed   11
Modern Buildings in Wessex   25
Thou Knowest My Sword   39
Blow Up   47
Red Hill   61
Imp Adrift   65
Protected by Occupation   72
Director's Cut   99
Ten Empty Rooms   113
Who Took Mary Cook?   117
An Oral History of the Greater London Exorcism Authority   130
Rainbow Pit   146
Alice Li is Snowed Under   152
Afterword: Council houses – haunted by something   163

Foreword

By David Southwell, author of the *Hookland Guide*

It is the lazy reviewer – or writer of forewords – that reaches for easy comparison. However, I will happily take that criticism and also any suggestion of self-obsession, because it is my view that there is a fair bit of crossover between *Municipal Gothic* and the county of Hookland. I am not talking of shared canon but rather familial ancestor DNA in terms of influence, as well as alignments of both strategies and values.

One area where I find common cause with Mr. Newman is in his refusal to treat his audience as anything less intelligent than himself. Ray often makes the reader work hard. He deals in implicit directions through the labyrinth, usual comfortable wool thread replaced with enigmatic scatterings of crushed rose petals. Yet it is those implicit directions that serve to engage, serve to make the reader complicit in the dooms of various characters. It all adds up to a rather satisfying narrative path through territories of terror.

I also feel a kinship between Ray's work and my aim with Hookland in his commitment to letting place be not only context, but character itself. My whole approach to writing changed when I took a BBC cab with J.G. Ballard along the Westway and his advice to me was: "Concentrate on place, nothing without a sense of it is ever any good." Not only in the glorious 'Modern Buildings of Wessex' but in 'Thou Knowest My Sword' and 'Who Took Mary Cook?', Ray invokes a definite sense of place and it blooming well helps deliver the goods. As someone always striving to give a feeling of life being lived as much in pub car parks, rows of shops in marginalised estates and the great forgotten acres of a rurality whose truths are often painful poverty and neglect, Ray's stories make me nod in gleeful recognition.

Things I have been gratified in being accused of when writing Hookland – 'an unpleasant bruising realism', 'slow terror', the committing of 'acts of psychic terror against the reader' – are all things I find in *Municipal Gothic* and take deep delight in. These are stories where pace propels you forward, but never rushes. These are stories you feel could be happening to that haggard bloke you see gulping whisky comfort at the bar. Stories happening to the people you are parked next to in the service station who are arguing when you stop for a toilet break and over-priced cup of sour coffee and who are still arguing 30 minutes later. People you have a sudden unbidden insight that they will never make it home. These are stories that haunt with a sense of relief that they haven't happened to you.

There are also some incredibly distinctive things in Ray's writing of which I and many other writers have cause to be jealous. He brings a quality that is rarely found in stories that have a genuine power to disturb – wit. Sharp, focused and never to the detriment of atmosphere, his deployment of raillery and even snark, gives his characters a depth of believability. We may not like Stewart Brayne's pisspuffinery, but we recognise it, and know him better for it. Ray's dialogue is full of the feral humour we engage in our own lives. In all legerdemain, the mastered art is not in the cleverness of the artifice, but the grace of execution. Grim chuckling that adds to the realism of horror is a hard trick to pull off and yet Ray makes it look like the easiest of things.

I feel kinship with Ray in our mutual fondness for experimental formats. Give us the chance to tell stories through liner notes, mail order shopping catalogues or promotional timeshare brochures for holiday destinations and we will both be racing to get our submissions in first. If you think bits of *Munic-*

ipal Gothic remind you of *The Phoenix Guide to Strange England County by County: Hookland or Repton* editions, I am happy to tell you at least one of Ray's stories presented here reminds me of my current secret project. We are not in competition, we are in community. A community where we are often inspired by the same sources and it should be known, often inspired by each other's work. It is important as an author having people you respect and whose work you like taking the same risks as you try to take. It is important to have those same people refusing to let horror be a ghetto of convention, who want the genre to bleed into every aspect of life as much as you do.

I often bang on about hauntology being a class issue. I will have paranormal researcher C. Josiffe say: 'The investigator who will be sniffy about "council house ghosts", who wants only National Trust spectres and ruin phantoms, is no friend to psychic research. The spirit snob is an enemy to the truth, a danger to our community.' I'll get Edwardian landscape punk C.L. Nolan ranting on about: 'The English aristocracy, living behind high walls and in stately, wood-panelled homes, would like the rest of us to believe their phantoms are dignified. All grey ladies and Sir What-the-Not. They don't like to tell of murdered maids, trapped chimney boys.' I do this because it is an issue that matters to me. There are damn few horror films told from a working class perspective that don't indulge in tired tropes, casually dismissive stereotypes. You do not need to read Ray's nuanced, insightful closing essay 'Council Houses – Haunted by Something' to know he's considered the territory, because *Municipal Gothic* is a glorious walk across it in itself.

Whether you discovered Ray Newman through the great online magazine *Horrified*, stumbled onto his website or brushed against him in social media, this is a collection to make you deeply glad of that initial encounter. Thirteen tales to puncture the psychic skin. Thirteen tales seeping out from the fault lines of our collective experience. Thirteen tales that refuse indolence, knowing you want the chance to be scarred, to be haunted. Read on and revel in one of the true powers of a good tale of terror – the chance to feel like your younger self when the world seemed so much more full of mystery and the engines of fright.

The Curse Follows the Seed

Sally was collecting a trolley from the far corner of the supermarket car park, where the shadows were deepest, when the black dog appeared and told her she would die before harvest was over.

'Why me?' she said.

The dog, which seemed at times to meld with the night, at others to glow, licked its teeth and yawned.

'Thou art the firstborn child of one in the line of Thomas Fletcher of Crediton and ever shall I hunt your kind, be they ever so far from the hills where he brought about the curse which marks you as surely as Cain was marked.'

'Don't be stupid,' Sally said with an awkward, honking laugh. 'There's no such thing as curses.'

The dog growled.

'Am I not proof of what weird things may be?'

A white van passed and its headlights multiplied in the spots of rain on Sally's glasses, dazzling her for a moment. When her sight cleared, the dog was gone.

She chewed her lip and stared at the bounding hedge with its green plastic rat traps and rotting pizza boxes. It would be difficult to concentrate on anything else, now, but her shift wouldn't be over until ten.

She stacked shelves smiling weakly and repeating the names over and over under her breath: 'Fletcher? Crediton?' It had the sound of the West Country about it. As had the dog, she noticed – a warm rumble, nothing like her own London Basin whine.

Her family had nothing to do with the West Country and weren't big on moving about. It had taken them two centuries to move from Kent into London and then back again.

'Crediton? Fletcher?'

She was a Dawes. Her mother was a Holdstock. She'd heard Paylis, Whiffin, Ovenden, but never Fletcher.

Driving home in her yellow hatchback, with the murmur of late night radio and the flat white of retail park light all around, she spoke aloud.

'Well, what does a silly dog know about anything anyway?'

The next morning, Sally put on her unicorn slippers and a toweling robe and went down to breakfast. Her mother, Ruth, was standing at the counter, busy with a knife on the chopping board.

'Morning, love. A bit of compote and some Greek yoghurt? Do wonders for your complexion, your regularity and your weight.'

Ruth was pale-skinned, blonde-haired and so slim she barely had hips.

Sally fell into her seat like an emergency sandbag.

'I'm not hungry,' she said.

'Even better,' said Ruth.

Sally, blinking behind smeared lenses, looked at her mother.

'Mum?'

'Yes, darling?'

'Have we ever been to Crediton?'

Ruth froze, first, then chopped with renewed intensity. Her face reddened, then drained of colour. She laughed, then frowned.

'Crediton? Never heard of it.'

Though Sally didn't rate herself a great reader of emotions – most faces looked as distinct to her as dinner plates – even she could tell that her mother did know Crediton and wasn't pleased that Sally had brought it up.

Sally fidgeted with the head of a plastic flower, stroking a gaudy, striped petal. She liked the texture.

Ruth continued chopping, dumping raw green pepper into the salad she was making.

'Mum?'

Ruth didn't respond.

'Do we know anyone called Fletcher?'

'No we bloody don't!' said Ruth, spinning to face Sally, holding the knife across her chest as if in self defense. 'What the bloody hell is this? Who've you been talking to?'

Sally blinked and chewed her lip.

'Nobody. It's nothing.'

'Look, I've got to go to work. When's your shift today?'

'Midday to nine,' said Sally.

'Well, do something useful with your morning, eh? The bathroom could do with a wipe-down for starters.'

'I was going to go to the library.'

'Why?'

'To look up Crediton.'

Ruth pretended she hadn't heard. She made a fuss about packing her handbag, attached her name badge to her blazer, and gave Sally an uncharacteristically intense kiss on the forehead as she swept out. The front door slammed and Sally sat alone in the house listening to its humming and ticking, heating and clocks.

From somewhere outside came the sound of a terrier yapping.

The black dog made its second appearance in Sally's own bedroom. She awoke to flickering blue light and the odour of sulphur, the air full of static.

Sitting upright in her single bed, she clawed around the bedside table until she found her glasses, which she put on with both hands. She stared into the hound's red eyes and yawned.

'Hello again.'

The dog whined and pulled itself into the shadows but said nothing.

'I know where Crediton is now. It's in Devon. Population 8,000. Main industries: dairy farming and tourism. Named after the River Creedy.'

She switched on the lamp.

The dog disappeared.

With a sigh, she turned the light off.

The dog, back, ran its dripping tongue around its teeth and gave a satisfied whine.

Sally picked up a book.

'I also got this. Can't read it in the dark but it's called *Devon Ghosts* and you're in it.'

The dog took a step closer and broke its silence.

'My tale is often told, rarely well, and never truthfully.'

'It says in this book that you haunt unbaptised babies.'

The dog gave a low growl that Sally felt more than she heard.

'I am servant to neither God nor Satan. My master, long absent, came from the far north, long before Christ, and cared not for church rituals.'

Sally sniffed and rubbed a finger under her cold, wet nose.

'What's this business about Fletcher, then?'

The dog seemed to expand in size, pulling shadow into itself to form new muscle.

'You are Fletcher's child and you will die,' it said, its breath hot and with the stink of burning peat.

'Yeah, I got that the first time. I'm not, though, that's the thing. But say if I was – how long would I have?'

'The days of ripening barley and the sharpening of scythes are upon us.'

'Soon then?'

'Soon.'

'Can I do anything about it?'

'The law is the law. Foreknowledge is fear and fear is punishment.'

The dog snapped its teeth together, bone on bone, and began to dissolve.

'One more question,' Sally said, swinging her feet over the edge of the bed.

Hovering between being and absence, the dog waited.

'What's his full name, this so-called Fletcher? His first name?'

The dog hesitated, fading further into nothing, and then as it crossed the threshold, half-spoke, half-howled the most prosaic name imaginable.

This time when Sally spoke to her mother, Ruth cracked. She let the melon baller fall to the counter with a clatter and flopped into a dining chair.

Sally polished her glasses on her pyjama top and waited.

'Your father and I tried very hard to have children.'

Nobody held a blank stare as solidly as Sally.

'But for some reason, it didn't work out.'

'Yeah?'

'He took too many hot baths, I expect. We looked into adopting—'

'Are you telling me I'm adopted?'

Ruth shook her head and winced.

'No. We looked into it, as I say, but your grandparents, both lots… Well, we just didn't think they'd accept an adopted kid. But someone told us about this clinic, see, where a very kind lady…' She began to cry, clasping bony hands over her quivering mouth.

Sally thought she ought to reach out and comfort her mother but that was a trick she'd never learned, somehow, so, instead, she waited, blinking, with her head tilted to one side – a gesture she understood sometimes conveyed sympathy.

'She was a pioneer in what they call donor insemination.'

'Sperm.'

Ruth tutted reflexively, then nodded.

'Well, yes, that.'

'Dad wasn't really my dad, then?'

'He was your father in every meaningful sense. He... We... You were very badly wanted.' Ruth sniffed and looked up at the ceiling, letting tears make tracks through the pale foundation that had barely dried on her cheeks.

'Is that why he left? Because I wasn't his?'

'He found it difficult. He didn't bond with you the way he was supposed to. I suppose I pushed him into it a bit. The clock was ticking, love – you know how it is.' She looked at Sally and almost rolled her eyes. 'Or maybe you don't.'

Sally tried to picture her father or, rather, Ruth's ex-husband. She didn't remember him but there were pictures – a lean, sharp-featured man with hair like Luke Skywalker.

'We didn't look much alike, now I think of it.'

'And you certainly don't get this from me,' said Ruth, gesturing at Sally's body.

'Why didn't you tell me before?'

'Well, what good would it have done? It would only have upset you when you were young – remember what you were like? Such a bloody crybaby. And now you've made it this far...'

She shrugged.

'Medical stuff, for starters,' said Sally, coming as close to raising her voice as she ever got. 'What if he's diabetic or, you know, I've, uh, inherited something else.'

Ruth tutted.

The Curse Follows the Seed

'Don't be such a drama queen. Have you got diabetes?'

'No.'

'Well then.'

'What do you know about him?'

'We know his name was Fletcher. He looked a bit like your dad because they tried to find a good match. No ginger babies for blonde parents or anything like that. And we know he did... Well, he did his business, with the–' She silently mouthed the word 'sperm' – 'in 1988.'

'That's ten years before I was born.'

'They keep it refrigerated, don't they? Like Häagen-Dazs. It lasts for ages.'

Her eyes narrowed and she brought her thin lips together into a wrinkled pout.

'Here, how did you find out? Who told you? Your Dad's not been in touch has he?'

Sally let her face settle back into blandness and just stared. Silence had always been her secret weapon.

After a few seconds, Ruth clapped her hands on her slim thighs, wiped a finger under each eye, and said, 'Fine. Whatever. Anyway, now you know, and I'd best get off to work.'

The third time, Sally summoned the dog herself. Somehow, she just knew how to do it: find a dark place – the basement was perfect – and whistle.

'Why have you brought me here?' the dog rumbled, conjuring its own spectral light. It patrolled with soundless steps the edges of the room, sniffing where mice had been running.

'Do you have a name? It would be easier if I could call you something.'

It growled.

'My master called me Old Rag.'

'Pleased to meet you, Rag. I know what's going on,' said Sally.

She pushed her plump hands into the pockets of her high-waisted jeans and shivered. The basement was cold and damp at the best of times but the dog seemed to suck up the last of the warmth.

'I'm technically this Fletcher bloke's daughter, but not really.'

'Tech-nic-ally?' Old Rag slavered over the new word as if it were a marrow-rich bone.

'He was a sperm donor. He donated his sperm, the clinic gave it to Mum and Dad so they could have me.'

At this, Old Rag fell to the ground and lowered his head upon his forelegs, like settling smoke. A deep whine came from his gut.

'Tell me more.'

'It's not complicated. They took his sperm, kept it cold for years, and put it inside my mother. Then I was born.'

'Not complicated?' said the dog with quiet astonishment. 'In older days, people were inventive in ways to nullify such curses. One Fletcher of old dressed the firstborn daughter of his line as a boy, and named her for a boy, but it mattered not: still I tore out her throat among the haystacks at Yeocombe in her twentieth year. Another rode to a far town where he seduced an idiot woman of low birth and left her there with child. Still, when the stars commanded it, I came for the girl and feasted on the meat of her lungs.'

Sally frowned and shifted the weight on her hips in such a way that she seemed almost to stamp a foot at the hound.

'Well, that hardly seems fair.'

Rag's red eyes dimmed.

'Fair?'

'If the curse is punishment, how does killing some young woman this bloke's never met, and doesn't care about, hurt him? I think he did you there, mate.'

The dog stood and began to prowl, circling Sally, more thoughtful than menacing.

'It is how it has always been done. A curse is a curse,' he said, though his voice had a distant, uncertain quality. He had lost his snarl.

'Well, it's a bloody stupid curse, then. Someone should have gone over the contract.' She stamped her foot again. 'Like I said, you've been done.'

Rag barked, full-throated, foul-breathed, gut-deep, and shook himself out of existence.

On her first break, after the lunchtime rush, Sally wandered out past the smoking area, beyond the bins and recycling skips, to the grassy slope between the store and the petrol station. As she sat in the sun eating a discounted egg and cress sandwich, she dialed a number she'd saved to her phone at the breakfast table that morning.

'Fletcher and Sons Heritage Builders, Angela speaking, how may I help you?'

The woman had a buttery country accent with soft, round vowels.

Sally, who avoided speaking on the telephone as much as possible, had to clear her throat before she could say at an audible volume, 'Can I speak to Nigel Fletcher, please?'

'May I ask who's calling?'

Tempted as she was to say, 'His firstborn child,' Sally simply gave her name.

'And what's the call regarding?'

'I'm calling about a dog.'

'Thank you, please hold,' said the receptionist.

Sally watched a seagull strutting nearby, pecking at cigarette ends in the stubble. After two bars of 'Build Me Up Buttercup' and two rings, a man's voice snapped in Sally's ear. It wasn't buttery at all, more like coffee grounds and broken eggshells.

'What kind of bloody joke is this? I'm not selling or buying a bloody dog.'

'I don't suppose you like dogs much, do you?' said Sally, not meaning to be arch.

'What do you mean by that?'

'I've been talking to a big black dog, or a sort of dog, called Old Rag.'

Nigel Fletcher switched the receiver from one hand to the other to buy a moment and then spoke in a strangulated whisper.

'Very fucking funny. Fucking hilarious. Who put you up to this? Jerry, I suppose? Well you can tell him this from me: he can harass me all he likes, he ain't getting one penny from the sale of that house.'

'I'm sorry, I don't know who Jerry is, or anything about a house.'

'Mum's house – Mum's bloody house!'

'I really have met Rag and he says I'm going to die because you're my… Because you… Because we're related.'

The breath whistled down Nigel Fletcher's nose and Sally heard the wet, wordless working of his mouth. The seagull, she noticed, was getting nearer.

'I told him I'm not your daughter, not really, so it doesn't count.'

'Of course you're not my–' he said in a near shout before stopping back down to a subdued hiss. 'Of course you're not my fucking daughter. What are you after? Because you're not getting a penny from the bloody house either.'

The Curse Follows the Seed

'Did you know about the curse when you donated?'

Sally heard a beep in her ear and knew the call had ended.

'Not had much luck with dads, have I?' she said to the seagull which pretended not to hear as it side-eyed her half-eaten sandwich.

That night, Sally sat up in silence, in darkness, waiting for Rag.

He materialised slowly this time, as if his battery was running low, and his blackness seemed less black than before. His eyes were dim, too.

'Firstborn, you have delivered the message of the curse to Fletcher.'

'You took your time. I was nodding off.'

Rag whimper-growled and slunk beneath the desk, among the cables and wires, beside the pink waste bin.

'It was simple, once. Bloodlines were bloodlines. Must you children of mud, you offspring of ash and vine, always make such obstacles?'

'Sorry,' said Sally, 'but it wasn't my bloody fault, was it? I just got born.'

Rag licked and breathed his butcher's bonfire stink.

'I call forth Black Edwin.'

'What?' said Sally, even as she became aware that there was now a large, musky goat in the room, regarding her with milky, dead eyes. Her room was narrow with only a few inches between the bed and desk and this creature occupied most of the remaining space.

'This is the child?' it said in a voice neither male nor female, glancing down at Rag, now trapped beneath the desk. Rag faded away and then, weightless, reappeared on the bed, standing over Sally, panting wisps of cold light.

'It is – the firstborn in the line of Fletcher.'

'But not his daughter, by his own declaration,' said the goat, like a barrister.

'How did you know that?' said Sally, pushing herself back against the headboard and grimacing. Her room smelled like a barn on fire.

'I attend always once I have found the scent,' said Old Rag. 'In other forms. In shadow. Invisible.'

'Fletcher has another child?' asked the goat.

Rag snorted.

'The second-born, a boy, his heir – Tyler Fletcher, of the city of Exeter.'

'I've got a brother?' said Sally. A smile broke across her face, then faded, then returned. She laughed and then laughed at herself laughing. 'I always wanted a brother.'

Then another thought occurred to her.

'When was Tyler born?'

The dog answered too quickly, 'It matters not.'

'No, seriously – when was he born?'

The curtains rippled in the breeze through the half-open window.

The goat answered.

'Nineteen-hundred and eighty-two.'

'So he was the first-born?'

'Your *seed* was first,' said Rag with a snort.

'But he was *born* first, right?' Sally laughed. 'We are complicated, aren't we, humans?'

Four eyes, two red, two pearl-white, stared at Sally. The goat kicked a heel. The dog panted.

'My decision is made,' said the goat at last. 'The days of the bough and pasture are behind us. We must adapt.'

Tyler Fletcher was vaping outside a bar on the edge of Cathedral Green when the lights went out. He watched the black lamp-posts flicker, dim and die one after another, and the shopfronts fall black, as if a wave had washed through.

He turned to go back into the bar and found it dark, too, and the door locked.

'What the fuck?'

He looked at the glowing face of his Swiss watch. It was suddenly, somehow, three in the morning. He exhaled one last, long mouthful of cinnamon-flavoured smoke and slipped the device into the pocket of his quilted jacket. A shiver took him over, from jowl to ankle.

Then a voice echoed across the cathedral square or, rather, a howl with words in it: 'Son of Fletcher! The curse is enacted this night!'

Who was that? Chidgey? Snegs? One of the lads. A wind up, of course. They'd probably dosed his drink or something – that would explain the missing hours and the headache. Massive, massive banter. Epic. It probably explained the dog, too – the thing as big as a horse that was running towards him quickly but slowly, heavy as stone but light as mist, across the green where, as a child, he'd danced around the maypole in beret and tunic.

Old Rag pounced, knocked him down, and for just long enough took corporeal form. Real fangs. Real claws. A tongue as rough as sandstone.

As the beast clamped onto his windpipe and carotid artery, Tyler Fletcher thought, 'Oh, so this is why Dad wouldn't let me have a dog.'

When Rag appeared to Sally the final time, his jaws seemed to sparkle with rubies or pomegranate seeds. He woke her by crying like a wolf from the back garden with its patio furniture and compost bin, threading her name into the infinite vowel. She opened the window and leaned out into the late summer air.

'Shush,' she hissed. 'People will hear you.'

'Not tonight, daughter of Fletcher. I am powerful now. I command light and sound and time and space.'

'Oh, that's good, isn't it?'

'Tyler Fletcher has been taken.'

Sally sighed.

'I never did get to meet him – my little brother! Or big brother, was it? I don't know.'

With that, she felt herself lift on the breeze and levitate from the window. She drifted, frictionless, out above the garden, until a soft, unseen wall stopped her above the dog. Its red eyes shone beneath her.

'But a curse is a curse, child of ash and vine, and now the second-born, first-seed child must die before the harvest is complete.'

She began to fall slowly towards the dog, like a drifting leaf.

Modern Buildings in Wessex

This guide is simply a list of the best post-war buildings I found on my travels in Wessex and nothing more. I have tried to be open-minded, objective and to express my opinions frankly. Aesthetics are less important to me than feeling and function and I ally myself with no particular school over another.

In general, the county has been slow to adopt modernism and many new buildings are, unfortunately, third-hand expressions of the neo-Georgian tendencies of the inter-war period. Although good work has been carried out by the County Council's own architects' department, and similar in-house teams at British Rail and the University of Exonbury, private practices from London have provided the impetus behind much that is most interesting.

Then, of course, there is Hälmar Pölzig – the nearest thing there is to local genius. Although scarcely an advocate for Pölzig's work, his influence on the modern architecture of Wessex since World War II can hardly be ignored. To that end, before embarking on this project, I dug up something many of my peers (with the notable exception of Dr Pevsner) had overlooked: Pölzig's 1965 article for *Magyar Építőművészet* which clearly established his buildings in Wessex as an interconnected body of work. A translation of this piece published in the *Architectural Journal* in 1966, though illuminating, for reasons unknown, omitted a vital passage in which Pölzig prescribes a particular order in which the nine buildings are to be visited. Out of respect for his conception, and perhaps with a mischievous desire to challenge his assertion that "a narrative is thus revealed", I have undertaken to follow his instructions.

Stewart Brayne, London, May 1968

St Leonard's School, Farrowbridge New Town
Verity and David Cohen-Bridges, 1958
School was never like this in my day: an austere arrangement of glass walls and raw concrete designed to bring the outdoors in and blow the cobwebs out of young minds. In London, it wouldn't register; here in the open country, it feels as wonderfully fresh as the local clotted cream. The hillside location is used to imply scale where, looked at objectively, none exists. These are humble buildings made grand only through the ingenious use of modern materials and, of course, the essential nobility of their purpose. Try telling that to the lads smoking behind the cricket pavilion, mind you.

Civic Centre and Central Court, Tonborough
Marnoch-Bracken Partnership and Wessex County Council Architects' Dept., 1965
The parallelepiped shape is bold, that's for sure, but what does it have to do with the purpose of the building? As an object, and an expression of craft, there's much to admire, from David Wynne's bronze statue of the Giant Gomegort to the clever use made of local brick to add character to outer walls that might otherwise seem intimidating or, worse, merely bland. Inside, however, it's the usual municipal linoleum, polished mahogany and plastic chairs that clutter up 90% of our public buildings and speak not so much of civic pride as cultural poverty. They wouldn't stand for it in East Germany.

Church of St Mary with St Francis, Shelmerston
Lang & Levis, 1961
A building that keeps its head when all around are losing theirs, insisting on calm despite its location on a busy junction of the A30. In lieu of Gothic, it offers only generosity – open doors,

unstained glass, bare walls of red brick that say, "A house of God I might be, but still a house for all that. Make yourself comfortable." Concrete is used only for the purely symbolic spire, for a cross (what a cross!) above the altar, and to provide unobtrusive, almost delicate structural support. If you can't have Wren or Gilbert Scott, this might just be the next best thing.

Gordon House, Higher Brent, nr. Tonborough
Hälmar Pölzig, 1957

The first of the nine and by no means a great work. A domestic house built on commission for the Scottish artist Cecil Gordon, it must have felt like a relic when new. Its suntrap roof, white rendering and banded windows speak of Mitteleuropa between the wars more than Britain Today! as the newsreels used to call it. There are distinctive touches, however, such as the abstract stained glass dividers that break up the single large room on the ground floor. Designed by Pölzig himself, they cast colourful, moving shadows that play thrilling tricks on the eyes. If you can stand in that room at sunset without spinning on your heels to see who's standing behind you, you're a better man than I.

Stannard Motor Works, Farrowbridge New Town
Bates, McAuley and Stolk, 1939

The earliest entry in this book, which is primarily intended as a survey of the post-war period, is this exercise in repetition and pure, unabashed functionalism. Because it was built quickly with war in mind – armoured cars were turned out in their thousands here – it anticipated the trend for modular construction by almost a decade, and is all the better for it. No pretension or cliches, only muscular, down-to-earth honesty. The glass roof in particular, designed to maximise light while minimising energy costs, is almost a work of art. If you get chance to see it from the air, do so, but just remember you're not over Zurich or Stuttgart as your eyes might lead you to believe.

Exmead Estate, Farrowbridge New Town
Wessex County Council Architects' Department, 1947-1956
When the human computers did their sums at the end of the war they concluded that there were too many people, not enough houses, and no money to build new ones. Or, at least, not to build good ones from brick or stone. The 3,000 houses at Exmead were constructed in four phases employing four different off-the-peg prefab designs from Laing, BISF, Unity and the Cornish Unit people. This piecemeal approach, quite unintentionally, apes the natural development of towns, providing enough variety to prevent monotony. The space is well used, too, with plenty of greens for recreation and a shopping precinct that traps the sun, inviting the housewives to stop and talk. Give it a few years and the spirit of the Blitzed slums of Bristol and Exeter will be revived here, mark my words.

King's Court, Tonborough
Hälmar Pölzig, 1958
The second stop on Pölzig's pilgrim trail is where the man's voice begins to sound loud and clear. A seven storey apartment block occupied primarily by Pölzig's fellow architects and artists desperate to kid themselves they live in London or Berlin, it applies the decorative tendencies of the Amsterdamse style to what would otherwise be a slab of glass and concrete. Instead of lions or big cats to guard the door, Pölzig commissioned Helen Sanders (b.1925-d.1958) to sculpt the *Aqrabuamelu* of Babylonian mythology – a pair of bare-chested, curly-bearded fellows with both wings and scorpion tails. Quite

a sight in the suburbs. Inside, there's more play with light and shadow, but wholly unsuccessful, unless the intention was to create dark corners and give the occupants headaches. Or perhaps only the truly sophisticated – the kind of people who also enjoy uncomfortable chairs and ugly paintings – can really appreciate the benefits of living on the verge of a nervous breakdown.

Bower Health Centre, Bridgeport
Steyer, 1951
Built in the altruistic frenzy of the immediate post-war period, with special assistance from the Ministry of Works, this is a fine building serving a real purpose. Doctor's surgery, optician, dentist and pharmacy are arranged around an open quad. The street front consists of two blocks joined by a colonnade. Murals by Alun Spencer (b.1921) depict, on one block, visions of healthy motherhood and plump children and, on the other, muscular working men and dignified ancients. Steyer later applied this clean, rather lofty style to similar buildings in Toxteth, Liverpool, and Selly Heath, Birmingham.

Theology Library, University of Exonbury
Hälmar Pölzig, 1959
The third Pölzig and the closest he ever came to a church. What do we know about Pölzig? That he was born in Stregoicavar, Austria-Hungary, in 1904; that he studied under Shandor in Vienna; came to Britain in 1938; and died in 1967. He wrote little, disdained the company of his peers, and was certainly never to be seen tripping out of the Windmill with Miss Diana Dors. Somehow, this building says more than any autobiography. The manipulation of light and shadow is here alright, especially in the long connecting corridors whose windowless, raw concrete walls bear oddly mobile abstract mouldings by

Glyn Jones (b.1919-d.1959). More than that, however, there's also a flexing of the muscles: this building is an expression of power. Try sitting at a reading table with a copy of the *Good News* and see how long it is before you start to feel weighed down, as if some god or other had his cyclopean thumb pressed between your shoulder blades. I was glad to leave even if I had the distinct sense that something of the building followed me down those dark medieval streets.

Queen Elizabeth Psychiatric Hospital, North Ham
Hälmar Pölzig for the National Health Service, 1960
Against my better judgement, two Pölzigs in a row, in the hope that the second might wash away the taste of the first. From the exterior, at least, a pointedly sane building: regular lines, curtain walling and a careful attention to the scale of human life that brings to mind Le Corbusier's Unité d'habitation in Marseille. The only sour note is a bronze by Pölzig himself that greets visitors at the top of the main drive. Although abstract – one of those fashionable dollops of dough with meaningful holes – it suggests bodies intertwined in an orgy. Or perhaps I have the kind of dirty mind they breed at English public schools. The interior is a different story, where Pölzig pulled a practical joke in bad taste, having Jerzy Sienkiewicz (b.1915-d.1960) cover the ceiling of the central hall with a fresco after Picasso, on the theme of the harvest moon. The lunatics – geddit? – must laugh into their straitjackets every night.

The Wessex Weaver, Exonbury
Courage Architects' Department, 1957
I was glad to visit this no-nonsense public house that condenses everything we've learned since the Beerhouse Act of 1830. It's not that it's beautiful – it's barely bigger than the houses that surround it, a near twin for the GP's surgery across

the square, all white wood and red brick. No, it's just that here is a place where a man can bathe in warmth and light, his back against a solid wall, and feel reassured that England still has its marbles. Avoid the pretentious lounge with its plastic frieze of basketmakers at work and head for the public bar where men with accents as ripe as old cheddar tell the dirtiest stories you'll hear this side of the officers' mess at Aldershot.

Severn Close, Tonborough
Bates, McAuley & Stolk, 1964
Around a courtyard, a set of sixteen Span-style bungalows bring the idea of the alms house into the 20th century. These are occupied by colonial pensioners and the sunny aspect, well-tended lawns and hardy palm trees must go some way to recompensing them for the loss of Empire. Don't be startled by what looks like one of Pölzig's suggestive sculptures on the hillside above: it's just a poor old wind-battered hawthorne, as I learned after a fifteen-minute hike and the destruction of my favourite brogues.

Linden Lea, St Hilary, nr. Exonbury
Hälmar Pölzig, 1961
A return to the domestic scale for the fifth stop as prescribed by Pölzig himself – a private house built for the industrialist Ernest Barclay. Barclay, who made his money in plastics, was an early advocate for Pölzig's work. In fact, so enamoured was he that he commissioned a portrait of the architect which hangs in the entrance hall at Linden Lea. The artist, Duncan Miles (b.1909-d.1961) was a peculiar choice having specialised in battleships but then Pölzig's face suggests something warlike and impregnable. Hard planes. Gunmetal eyes. As for the house, this three storey villa is, despite the name, no country suntrap – it wouldn't look out of place on the Maginot line or with an anti-

aircraft gun on the flat roof. Employing a special treatment of Pölzig's own invention, the raw concrete of the exterior is deeply, mesmerisingly black.

The Madding Crowd, Tonborough
Brocklehurst & Walsh for Watney Mann, 1966

A mural depicting the life of Thomas Hardy is a colourful addition to this confidently brash steakhouse off the A30. I wonder what the old misery himself might have made of the waitresses in 'rustic maiden' costumes and the endlessly flowing keg beer. The circular structure is the primary point of interest, along with the exposed beams – real structure, not hunks of firewood glued in place to titillate the nostalgists. The atmosphere, which too few pub designers really think about, is one of pleasing ordinariness – there's no Transylvanian angst here among the arctic rolls and jacket potatoes. Or at least, there shouldn't be, but once you've seen that face you start to see it everywhere.

Fairfield House, Sandford
Hälmar Pölzig for Wessex County Council, 1963

A simple eleven storey point block with associated shopping arcade, in red brick with white rendering on side walls. Ostensibly fresh and logical, presumably under close management by the WCC Architects' Department, Pölzig cannot help but be original. Here, his genius manifests in a roof garden after Le Corbusier. Abstract concrete shapes by an acolyte of Pölzig, Giancarlo Palaggi (1936-1963), are designed to deaden or amplify sound creating eerie pockets of complete silence and moments of deafening intensity. That they also resemble looming monastic figures is a remarkable coincidence. Sadly, the garden was closed only months after opening when a young resident fell to her death, and can only now be viewed by special permission.

Central Station, Farrowbridge New Town
B.R. Western Region Architects Department, 1962
A similar plan to Plymouth but more frank and less concerned with signalling its own importance. To the street, a glass-fronted block with B.R. offices above; a spacious concourse with shops; and six platforms with airy weatherboarded waiting rooms. The whole thing is a machine engineered to cope with rush-hour and matchday, yes, but also to make the most of views across open country to the west – one could really enjoy a long wait for a delayed train here. The space, the tranquility and the sheer institutional orderliness of it all are a tonic, and the very opposite of Pölzig's exercise in subtle torture. Of course I saw him here, too, as a shadow in the underpass between platforms, agitating in the periphery. It's the drink, my wife would say, but the drinking is a symptom, not the cause.

Sandford College of Art, Sandford
Hälmar Pölzig, 1965
On a hilltop outside town, two parallel slabs face each other across a courtyard with the main administration block in the form of a pyramid – the kind of 'out there' gesture to which only the polo-neck, French cigarette smoking, pop art crowd would ever agree. Its glass upper houses a gallery with offices and dining hall below. The slabs are home to workshops and lecture halls. It all seems quite innocent until you try to shelter from the wind and realise what Pölzig is up to: there is nowhere to hide. The structures are arranged to funnel the gale so that you forever feel as if giant paws are batting you about. Inside, the wind whines through window-frames and seems to set up a

vibration in the very brick. I'd have blamed shoddy workmanship or negligence in the case of any other architect but everything the Hungarian does is deliberate. The student art on display suggests his influence, too, subconscious or otherwise – all shadow, staring eyes and alien forms.

The Ship at Anchor, Sandford
Whitbread Architects Dept., 1967
A nautical pub for a landlocked town, with portholes, lobster pots and a bar in the shape of a longboat in the saloon. One whisky, two whiskies, six pints of sweet Wessex draught bitter, but somehow I'm still in Pölzig country. I ought to say something about the faux-lighthouse and clever curve of the structure, oughtn't I? But who cares. It's a pub – a bright, friendly pub with all the drink in the world, that I never want to leave. Three whiskies, two more pints, because outside, night has fallen, and I know he is the night.

Ministry of Labour, Exonbury
Hälmar Pölzig, 1966
When the Government decided to build a great western outpost for its slave driving department, Pölzig bid for the job, and got it. His biggest building to date, this two-wing, twelve-storey monstrosity dominates a part of the city that was marshland two decades ago. He met the specifications, that's all the bureaucrats care about – never mind the sheer bloody horror of the place. Inspired, if inspired is the word, by the Great Ziggurat of Ur in Iraq, it stands above and apart from everything else. Its concrete walls are already turning black and weep green. The windows point downward, ostensibly to provide soft light and protect the occupants from the sun, but they resemble nothing so much as the disdainful eyes of some great, impossible beast. The Man from the Ministry who gave me a tour

seemed proud of the 'unique' layout of the structure: "It's not just a box like so many modern buildings," he said, and indeed it isn't. One wing is hexagonal, the other octagonal, and on some floors they overlap. Because of the slope, what is the ground floor at the front entrance becomes the second floor by the time you reach the back. Fluorescent lights don't seem to reach the corners of the rooms so it always feels like twilight. There are more of those whining windows. As a result, the staff look lost and unwell. It's an almost perfect device for the slow demolition of the soul.

Central Library, Exonbury
Wessex County Council Architects Department, 1954
Festival balconies, mosaic finish, slatted wooden staircases, high windows, Scandinavian furniture – you know the drill. The important thing is, you can sit there all day under bright light, in silence, and feel truly warm for once. And they have microfilm readers. Do you know how many members of Ministry of Labour staff have killed themselves in the past two years? The national rate is something like twenty per 100,000. At the Ministry, with 600 staff, there have been fourteen. The Art School at Sandford isn't far behind but then I suppose art students are prone to melodrama. Here's something else: Pölzig had a frieze designed for the front of the Ministry building that they refused to mount. It was called 'The Dignity of Labour' and was cast in concrete by Bill Morris. Do you know what happened to Bill Morris? No, nor do I. Nor does anybody. The frieze ended up in the foundations of the M5 motorway. There are no photos and they wouldn't let me see the memos.

The Fox & Horses, Stoke Barton, nr. Exonbury
Alfred Hilton for Greenleaf & Smith, 1953

A pub built to serve a private overspill estate and one designed with great sensitivity and honesty. Two-storey house, domestic in style and scale, with a single-storey public bar to one side and a separate children's room and play area. And by God, it's good to hear children playing and to be surrounded by young parents in a neighbourhood the locals call Pram City. He didn't reach here, he can't penetrate here – it's simply too wonderfully prosaic. But, you see, I say that, and then I see him across the lounge, crabbed hand on cane, raising a glass in my direction. What can I do but raise a glass in return? I tip whisky down my throat, grimace through the burn and when I look again, he's gone, which only seems reasonable given that I read his obituary in *Architectural Review* which is what set me thinking about the blasted man at all.

The Wessex Motel, Exonbury bypass, Latchford
Sir James Phelps for Forte, 1966

A bed, polyester curtains in mustard, whisky miniatures from the bottle. I don't suppose it can be put off any longer, the final Pölzig. Is there anything to stop me getting into my car, pointing it in the direction of London and driving until I'm home? Home: a blessedly unhaunted Georgian house in Chelsea with two bays and not a single diversion from the pattern book. It's absurd, isn't it, to be afraid of a building? Except that's not what scares me – it's the strength of my desire to see the culmination of his experiments. To pay homage to a man I've come to admire. To serve, I suppose you might say, the man I've come to think of as master. No doubt there's something Freudian in it but that's probably true of most architectural criticism – all that swooning over finials and domes.

Combe Stephen flyover, nr. Tonborough
Wessex CC Architects' Dept., 1962

Part of the scheme to ease traffic through Combe Martin, a pretty Wessex village, this firm but sensitive addition to the landscape compliments rather than compromising the wetlands beneath. It also offers a view of the Residenzia Pölzig – a black finger penetrating the sky above pine trees planted in 1948 to replace ancient woodlands stripped bare as part of the war effort. It's all there in those few storeys of concrete and glass, every bit of the man's artistry, and it's one in the eye for the forces of repetition and British deference that dominate the shires. What it says, somehow, is this: mankind is sick and the cull must come; come, now, and be culled. Does the National Trust, which now has custody, understand this? I doubt the retired majors and interfering cardigan-knitters will ever open it to the public at any rate.

Rezidencia Pölzig, Combe Stephen
Hälmar Pölzig, 1968

Scorpion-men, ghosts trapped in glass, the very shape of the thing a lie – tricks of light and forced perspective. But try telling that to the lads smoking behind the Edwardian cricket pavilion. It's bold, that's for sure. Ignoble purpose. But try telling that to the lads. Unclear and illogical. Sober blocks, tall slabs, tough-minded to the point of cruelty. Muscular energy, a twist of the arm, a boot in the face. A wholly successful pretence, the best practical joke in architecture since St Paul's Cathedral, mark my words. They wouldn't stand for it in East Germany. But try, just you try, telling that to the muscular lads with their tough-minded cast concrete beams behind the cricket pavilion. No corners have been cut – a pure confident expression of pure confidence, expressed confidently. Mark my words – just you mark my words.

Municipal Gothic

★ ★ ★

Stewart Brayne (1931-1968) was an influential and irreverent architectural critic and an advocate of bold Continental modernism over what he saw as the meek British compromise of the Festival of Britain school. He wrote county guides to Gloucestershire and Dorset for this series and at the time of his death was planning a comprehensive study of buildings in Denmark. This monograph is based on notes he left behind. It was edited for publication by the staff of the British Institute of Architects and the Wessex Polytechnic University School of Building.

Thou Knowest My Sword

A new ordnance factory on the marsh means new workers – skilled people from Woolwich, Waltham Abbey and Enfield. New workers means a new housing estate. And a new estate means a new telephone box. That is why, on a summer afternoon as hot as chip grease, Ted Gunntripp is creaking along the Wickberrow Road on his bicycle.

Ted is young, red cheeked and bluntly handsome – certainly fit enough to fight but his expertise with telephones has spared him. His GPO cap is tipped back on his head to let out the steam. He is whistling 'The Biggest Aspidistra in the World', sending his own signal out across the stinking, algae-covered rhynes and dry fields. Flies, bees and crickets accompany him in microtones. The tall grass ripples gentle applause.

He labours up Horsland Hill, over cowpats flattened into the asphalt by military traffic, and stops at the top to look down on Widdington.

'Bloody hell,' he says aloud.

The village is still there – a spire, some tufts of thatch, the half-timbered inn – but it has acquired a growth. Three hundred prefabricated steel bungalows are arranged in crescents and rows, like teeth crowded in a child's mouth. Shaking his head, he remounts the pedals and freewheels down the hill, still whistling.

He passes a sign. Black paint obscures the name of the village in case German paratroopers should land nearby: WELCOME TO _____, SITE OF THE BATTLE OF _____, 1643.

A barn, a gate, a well and then the first of the prefabs, the second, the third, the fourth. They aren't finished, just shells awaiting windows, doors and rust-proof paint. Their corrugated walls cause the sound of his bicycle wheels to reverberate tightly.

'This here is a gal darn ghost town, Tex,' he mutters.

He makes a six-shooter with his fingers and blasts imaginary holes in the metal of the houses. They groan and creak in the hot breeze.

After two minutes cycling up one unnamed road after another, Ted finds the centre of the new estate. It has its own village green (flowerbeds pending), a prefab shop (empty), a postbox (sealed with a plate) and a brand new, bright red K6 telephone box (not yet connected). The latter is Ted's job. He trundles to a halt and skips off the bike leaning it against the post box.

The telegraph pole is in the centre of the green as if designed for children to dance around. It is already connected to the main line on the Wickberrow Road. Wires sag out from its crown to the pub in the village, to the police station and to the manor house where the War Office is up to something, God knows what. Squinting into the blue sky, Ted slaps the timber. He puts on his climbing belt and toolbag and begins his ascent.

Halfway up the pole, he feels a chill and pauses. Something in the air has changed. He wonders if thunder might be on the way.

He looks over to the road, then across the floodplain, then down at the new village green.

He blinks.

He frowns.

He shivers.

There is somebody there – the first person he has seen since leaving the depot on the edge of town.

The stranger's face is turned away so Ted can't see it. Sun glints off the silver sheen of an oversized soldier's helmet. Not a Tommy's tin hat and not a Yank chamber pot, either. Definitely not a Kraut, thank goodness. French, maybe? The uniform is a dull brown, coarsely cut, with high black boots. Ah, Dutch, thinks Ted, or Belgian. There must be a camp nearby, in one of those blank redacted zones on the GPO map. He isn't convinced but it's an explanation that will do for now.

'Lovely day, ennit?' Ted shouts.

The man doesn't acknowledge the call.

Ted tries again: 'Bonjour, mon ami! Howdy, pardner!'

Nothing.

Ted shrugs.

'Suit yourself, then,' says Ted quietly.

He tips back his cap and squints. The stranger is rooted to the spot but isn't still. He is holding something in his gloved right hand. Light glances from it. It's not a gun. It might be an infantry shovel, for digging foxholes. No, hold on, is it…? It is. It's a bloody sword.

The stranger's hand twists and tightens around the grip of the sword. In the silence, over the whisper of the wind, Ted thinks he can hear breathing – panting, perhaps. It is as if the man is waiting for something and Ted's eyes drift upward, scanning the green and the new street that runs away from it towards the old village. There is nothing, nobody, no cats or squirrels, not even a bird. Odd, that, Ted thinks – no birdsong and no insects either.

Ted looks at the man one last time. Doing so makes him feel panic, a kind of vertigo, or something like seasickness. He snatches his eyes away and looks up into the sky. After a moment, he breaks free from his own inertia and continues to climb. At the top of the pole, he takes a leather loop from his belt and lashes it around the timber. He lets it take his weight and sits back in the cradle. He looks down again. The stranger has gone. He feels relieved but glances around – where has he gone? He isn't on the road.

Ted's bike is where he left it, though, so at least the stranger isn't a thief.

'Can't spend all day worrying about Belgians,' he mutters, scowling.

Ted puts on insulated gloves and takes a loop of rubberised cable from his belt. With practiced dexterity he strips the rubber away to free a strand of copper wire which he fixes to the insulator with five twists of his pliers. He then lets the cable drop to the ground, spinning and whipping as it goes. He removes his gloves and stuffs them in his knapsack. He begins his descent.

He grunts and sweats as he goes. It is always harder than going up, all the linesmen know that. Every foot or so he stops to tack the cable in place with steel brackets, a small hammer and a mouth full of nails.

Halfway down he feels an electric prickling on the hairs of his neck. The air feels thicker and warmer. He knows, then, that he must look at the green.

The soldier is there again in the same place, in almost the same stance, except that, now, the sword is extended, ready for battle.

Ted blinks slowly. He feels as if he is trapped on flypaper.

He hears a sound, like the rush of blood or the movement of the tide, and looks up towards the horizon. He can't see troops but can certainly hear them – boots on dry earth, locked in step.

The soldier below takes a step back, then forward again. He tightens his grip on the sword and speaks: 'Oh Lord, thou knowest my sword must labour this hour. Forget me not if I forget thee. Give strength to my blade–'

Loud, now, the roar of the advancing army seems to sound from just beyond the nearest row of bungalows. Armour and spurs. A dull, penetrating drumbeat. Ted doesn't know whether to retreat upward or fly down and away on his bicycle.

'–defend us in battle–'

The sunlight seems to blacken as during an eclipse.

'–protect us against the snares and wickedness of the devil–'

Ted shakes his head, breaks free from the confusion, and all but falls the rest of the way, flushed and panting. Splinters pierce his fingers. As his boots hit the grass he uncouples his climbing belt and stumbles away. He trips and falls, landing heavy on the road. The wind is punched from his lungs by the impact.

He gasps, panicked, until he realises he can hear the five-note song of a wood pigeon and, beyond that, the distant growl of an RAF transport plane. A bee as big as a shilling piece dances past, wings humming.

The air is warm again, the sky bright. There are no soldiers. He hears no shouting.

He takes control of his breathing and wipes sweat from his face.

After another minute has passed, he props himself up on his elbows and bends a knee. He feels the cleansing warmth of the sun on his face and chest. He coughs and takes a cigarette from the packet in his tunic pocket. He lights it with a match and smokes it with great satisfaction.

He hears a new sound, then – the cable, still loose, slapping against the pole as it moves in the wind. His smile fades.

He doesn't want to go up there again.

That's daft, he says to himself.

He scratches his head beneath his cap.

'Well, cable's got to be done, boy, or it's curtains for you,' he says aloud.

He climbs to his feet and dusts down his uniform. He picks up his belt from the base of the pole and reconnects it. Then he spits in hands, rubs them together, but can't quite bring himself to begin to climb. He looks at the green – empty.

As long as there are birds singing, he thinks, and as long as the sun is shining like this, like gold, not lead, then I'll be alright.

He grabs the pole and, with a grunt, sets off.

The landscape beyond the new estate looks perfect and peaceful. He doesn't need to go above halfway – the cable could be tacked well enough from below that point. But it has become a matter of principle. Guntripps ain't cowards. Guntripps ain't afraid of nothing. He hoists the belt another foot, lifts himself on the protruding peg.

He feels the change at once. Suddenly, it is like looking through a lens or prism – everything the same, but different. The soldier is back.

Now, though, he is no longer standing in defiance. He is laid out on the ground, his plain chestplate buckled and torn open. His face is black, bruised, washed with dry blood. His teeth show like pearls in river mud. The sword is gone.

Ted looks for a long time.

He thinks about his brother, Jack, lost on the bottom of the Atlantic. He recalls the faces of the lads from school who didn't come back after Dunkirk.

'Tough luck, old chap,' he says to the long-dead man on the ground, his voice low and soft.

Then he takes out his hammer and a fistful of nails and, with shaking hands, sets about tacking the cable in place. 'For years,' he calls into the silence, shyly, 'we had an aspidistra…' He works his way down the pole, singing in lieu of his own protective prayer, until the gloom lifts.

On the ground, he uncouples. He lights another cigarette and stares across the green. With one hand in his pocket he strolls across the grass. The earth feels solid beneath his boots.

Thou Knowest My Sword

He reaches the place where the soldier had been standing, then lying. There is no shiver along his spine, no lightning bolt, no feeling of cold or dread. He kneels and places a palm flat on the ground. Just English soil. Perhaps there are bones below, scraps or rusting armour, but they don't speak to him. He looks up at the immense blue sky and sighs.

Springing up, he shakes his head.

'Sunstroke, probly,' he says aloud, then laughs, mockingly. 'Fancy getting addled like that by a bit of sunshine.'

It takes thirty minutes to dig the cable into the ground. He uses an extendable shovel to remove neat divots, placing them at the side of the narrow trough. Then he runs the cable into the box through the base, twisting and screwing the copper wire into place. He repairs the turf, stamping it down with his boots, then takes a clipboard from his satchel, licks his pencil and ticks several items. The next is 'Dial tone check'.

Whistling softly, he steps into the box and props the clipboard on the shelf. He takes hold of the handset, dabs the cradle and lifts the virgin Bakelite to his ear. The hum satisfies him and he marks it off on his checklist. Then he inserts a black fingernail and drags the dial to zero. It purrs back into place. The dial tone cuts with a click. Dead silence.

'Operator?'

Nothing.

'GPO line check, love. Are you going to answer or what?'

He hears unsteady breathing, the catch of a word in a dry throat.

Ted rolls his eyes.

'Speak up, darling – I can't hear you.'

'Oh Lord...' comes a hesitant whisper. A man's voice, distorted and crushed. 'It is so cold here.'

Ted drops the handset. It falls on its cord and slams against the wooden panel at the back of the box. Leaving tools, bicycle and clipboard behind, he runs between the prefabs, up Horsland Hill, towards the sun.

Blow Up

Mel had never met Rory until the moment he got into the back seat of the Range Rover. He was just as Aidan had described him: 'Built like an outside shithouse, shiny as a new tuppence.' Despite all the muscles Rory had the face of a teenager, as plooky as it was chubby. She didn't fancy him in the slightest.

'Alright,' Rory said.

'Alright,' replied Darek from the passenger seat, making eye contact only through the prophylactic of the rear-view mirror.

'Show us the guns, then,' said Mel. 'Let's see what we're paying for.'

She looked over her shoulder, snapped her chewing gum.

Rory smirked and pulled back the sleeve of his T-shirt. He made a snake of his arm with his fist for the head and popped a bicep, making it dance in time with the music on the stereo.

'Very pretty,' said Mel. 'You know the drill, yeah?'

'I do indeed.'

'You've done this before?'

'I know the drill.'

Mel looked him up and down one last time, grinding the gum between her teeth. She'd asked around and heard some worrying things about Rory's attitude. It was too late to pull out now, though, and anyway, they had no choice. Aidan was bankrolling, and Rory was his nephew. Some poor bastard had to break him in and Aidan had decided it would be Mel, so that was that.

Rory leaned forward, pushing his big head between the rests of the front seats. The smell of synthetic musk and lime shower gel caught in Mel's throat.

'You the gasman, then?'

Darek nodded.

Rory waited for more but it didn't come. He shrugged and sat back.

Mel drove with her hands at ten to two on the wheel. Darek gave occasional directions and stared out of the window, his pearl-pale skin tight around his narrow jaw. Rory plugged in headphones that leaked the claps, snares and synthesisers of grinding R&B. There was no conversation because they didn't know each other and didn't want to. They all knew Aidan but there was no point in talking about him. Loose lips sink ships.

They were on the M4 heading west when Rory spoke again.

'I need a slash.'

'I'll stop at the next services.'

'Just pull over on the hard shoulder. I'll only be a minute.'

'Aren't you house trained? We'll wait until the next services.'

'Ain't very gangster, is it, following all the rules?'

Darek glanced at Mel, just barely rolling his blue eyes. Typical muscle, he said without words.

Mel smiled diamond-hard at Rory in the rear-view mirror.

'And what if the feds see us pulled over, and you with your little 'roid-shrunken cock out sprinkling the verge, and decide to have a look in the boot?'

Rory flushed, half angry, half embarrassed.

'It ain't shrunk, love. You can have a look if you like.'

'When they see us, and they see Darek's kit, what do you think will happen? Have you noticed that I've not gone over sixty-five the whole way? We go slow, keep our heads down, and piss where we're supposed to.'

'Yeah,' said Rory. 'I know. I was only joking.'

'Oh, right. Very funny.'

Darek smirked.

They came off the motorway as scheduled at a little after nine in the evening.

'If you need to eat, eat,' said Mel.

Darek shook his head. He didn't look as if he ever ate.

'Um...' said Rory.

'Need some protein, son?' said Mel. 'One of those special milkshakes you lot like?'

'Any chance of a Maccy D?'

'No,' said Mel. 'Too many cameras.'

Darek sniffed and looked at his chipped fingernails. Then he reached between his legs and pulled up a carrier bag full of sandwiches and chocolate bars. He passed it back to Rory who began to rummage like a puppy in a kitchen bin.

They passed a truck stop, floodlit and busy. There was a row of articulated lorries from Romania, Spain, Poland, Italy, Bulgaria – everywhere – and a Portakabin beyond. Its lights glowed pale yellow and the windows were fogged.

Then Mel saw a flash of white, the gleam of a high visibility jacket and a blink of blue light – a police motorbike had appeared from the other side of the Portakabin and was cruising across the cracked concrete towards the exit.

She had two choices: keep driving and let it fall in behind them, or stop and let it out. Either way, he'd notice them, and they didn't want to be noticed.

Darek noticed the car lurch as she dabbed the brakes, then changed her mind. He looked up and saw the policeman.

'Chicken and stuffing is a fucking good flavour of sandwich, innit?' said Rory, spitting wet crumbs into the front of the car.

'Too salty,' said Darek. 'No fibre.'

Mel accelerated and let the bike drop in behind.

As they followed the road into town, Mel's eyes kept darting back to the mirror.

Yes, there he was – a white motorbike behind a white headlight, hanging back but definitely following.

Darek muttered, 'What do we do?'

'What?' said Rory, looking up from the cardboard box of his second sandwich with mayonnaise around his mouth. They ignored him.

'Call it off?' said Darek. 'He'll get our plates.'

The bike was getting closer all the time.

'Plates won't matter in an hour's time. Chill. Trust me.'

Then the bike's blue light began to flash, lighting up the car with its slow, cold strobing.

'Oh, no,' said Rory. 'Five-oh.'

'*Kurwa*... If he gets a look in the back, we're screwed,' said Darek.

'I know.'

As they approached a roundabout on the edge of an industrial estate the bike pulled alongside on the right and the policeman waved a gauntlet, instructing Mel to pull over.

She tightened her grip on the wheel.

'I'll talk,' she said, pulling the car to a smooth halt.

The motorcyclist stopped but hung back.

'He's going to call in our number,' said Darek. 'Any second.'

'What are you going to do?' asked Rory, his voice cracking like an over-the-hill choirboy.

Mel sighed.

'Hold tight, lads.'

In one liquid move she jammed the car into reverse and the Range Rover roared backwards into the motorcyclist, then over him, with an abattoir crunch.

She braked and the car rocked to a stop in the middle of two lanes.

'Muscles,' she said. 'You're up.'

'What the fack?' said Darek. His voice was shaky.

'Jesus Christ,' said Rory. 'Jesus fucking Christ.'

'Rory, mate, calm down. Get out and chuck him and the bike in the ditch.'

'Fucking hell – why did you do that?'

'Rory…'

'Why me? Why do I have to do it?'

'The only reason you're here is manual labour. Now quick before someone comes.'

'Fuck sake… Don't go without me, alright?'

Mel watched the road looking out for lights. It was a small town, late, and the nearby factories were all closed. Still, the truck stop had been busy.

Darek shook in his seat, working his leg up and down like a pump, muttering.

Rory squatted and lifted the policeman as if he were a sack of flour. He tossed him with a spin into the filthy water at the side of the road, like the final move in a wrestling match.

Darek said something in Polish and shook his head.

The bike, Rory dragged, kicking up sparks, finishing it off with a few kicks. It slid over the edge and boomed as it bellyslapped the surface.

Mel had the car moving before he'd even closed his door.

'Que sera sera,' said Darek. He didn't sound convinced.

'Let's finish the job,' said Mel, sounding calmer than she felt. Her heart wanted to rattle loose.

At a big junction in town, between a shuttered DIY store and a boarded-up cinema, she stopped for a red light. That was when Darek yawned, smoothly unclipped his seatbelt, opened his door and got out of the car.

'Okay then, see you around.'

He slammed the door and walked away.

The lights changed and washed Mel's face green.

'Darek, come back. Darek, you prick!'

Darek didn't reply or turn around. He slipped into an alleyway beside the cinema and faded to black.

She drove on.

No gasman, no job. No job, no pay. No pay and probably, a tightening in her gut reminded her, at the very least a beating. Nothing compared to what they'd do to Darek if they ever caught him, though.

She looked at Rory in the rear view mirror. He looked more childlike than ever, petrified and sweaty, but his lips were moving as he worked out a thought.

'We're in trouble now, aren't we? That filth in the ditch and not being able to do the job and that.'

'Yeah,' said Mel. 'We are. And don't think your uncle will let you off easy.'

'Shit,' said Rory. He chewed a nail. 'I can do the gas,' he said. 'I know how.'

Mel pulled into a layby outside a row of tatty shops. She switched off the engine and put her head in her hands on the steering wheel.

'Honest, I can do it. How hard can it be?'

He had a point. It wasn't nuclear physics. Darek wasn't a genius – just a bloke who'd had a bit of practice. All his kit was still in the boot, too, including the red gas canister. She pictured success, the two of them returning to London with the cash, splitting Darek's forfeited cut between them, and extra credit for triumph in adversity.

'Fuck it, why not,' she said.

It went quickly from that moment.

She pulled on a lightweight balaclava. Rory did the same, his pink lips poking through the too-tight Lycra in a forced pout. The supermarket was a short drive away, over a railway bridge and beside a quiet housing estate. Rory used cutters to snip through the chain on the security gate. No longer driving carefully, Mel flew across the car park and spun the Range Rover to a stop next to the row of three cash machines.

Rory tumbled out and grabbed the gas tank with its length of pipe. The tank rang out as it hit the asphalt.

He lumbered across to the cash machines and forced the pipe into the card slot on the one in the middle. Then he jogged back and spun the valve to release the gas.

Mel tried to remember how long Darek had let the gas run last time – ten seconds, maybe? Twenty?

'Hurry up,' she shouted.

Rory gave her the thumbs up and reached into the boot a second time, pulling out a marine flare gun. It was already loaded.

'Turn the gas off,' said Mel.

Rory didn't hear her. He pointed the gun sideways, striking a ludicrous gangster pose, and laughed as he pulled the trigger.

She hammered her foot down and shifted as quickly as she could, clipping flowerbeds and kerbs as she went. Tools and equipment scattered behind her from the open boot.

The cashpoint exploded, then the gas canister, and in the bloom of white light she saw Rory being thrown through the air.

He wasn't in one piece.

Alarms were sounding and lights came on in every house along the road. Chunks of blazing metal landed across the car park. Struggling to keep the Range Rover on course she swerved out of the gate and turned left, away from town, towards open country.

Mel didn't cry, she hadn't cried since she was eight years old, but she wanted to.

Salobreña on the Mediterranean coast near Granada was boring, especially out of season, which is exactly why Mel chose it. Among the Germans, Danes and Dutch there were a few British expats but not the sociable sort. They sat in their beachside apartments watching waves wash over the plastic patio furniture of the cafes, reading the *Daily Mail* and binging on repeats of *Homes Under the Hammer.*

It suited Mel. She was too old for clubbing and had decided to let herself become middle-aged, at last. Nobody from London would recognise her, she was sure, with her hair left to its natural grey, no make-up and shapeless, sensible pastel clothes. There was nothing flash about her flat, either, or the decade-old Honda parked outside.

Aidan wouldn't waste too much time looking for her, anyway. It wasn't as if she'd got away with any money and, she'd heard on the grapevine, Aidan blamed Darek more than her. He had the boys hunting the Pole everywhere from Bulgaria to Thailand, where Darek had always claimed to have a wife and kids.

Most days, Mel slept in. She ate breakfast alone – bread, olive oil, tea – overlooking the courtyard with its benches and palm trees. At lunchtime she walked the length of the promenade and back again, past sleeping hotels and restaurants with folded awnings and curtained windows. After lunch, she watched Spanish TV, or at least had it on while she stared vaguely toward the screen, hoping but failing to improve her Spanish. At four in the afternoon she'd open a bottle of wine and drink it slowly until it was time to go to bed, reading one of the tattered paperbacks that had come with the flat.

She thought about Rory all the time. They'd known each other for less than ten hours and she hadn't much liked him but the image of his plump, boyish lips pushed out by the balaclava was a constant overlay, especially when she closed her eyes.

It wasn't until near Christmas that she saw him in person, though.

Dozing in her armchair, an inch of supermarket rioja left in her glass, she said his name out loud and woke herself. The apartment seemed to buzz with some dog whistle energy. She downed the last of the wine and took the few steps to the window over the courtyard. A warm wind was shaking the palms and blowing a disposable coffee cup in circles around the *petanca*. Rory, in his dumb bulk, was just stood there, looking up at her as if serenading – except he couldn't really look, or sing, because he was headless.

Mel never cried and she never screamed. All that had been bred and beaten out of her. She did, however, feel sick, not only at the sight of the raw, blackened stump of his neck but because she knew what it meant: he blamed her for his death and was going to haunt her.

It was worse than Aidan's boys turning up. At least then she'd have a chance to grab the gun from the chest of drawers by her bed, or to run. Even if they got her, she'd be at the bottom of the sea before morning. God knew how long this nonsense was going to last.

She opened the window a little further.

'Now, what the fuck do you want?'

A light went on across the courtyard and a shape appeared in silhouette.

Rory, obviously, said nothing, but swayed or perhaps shimmered.

She noticed that his clothes were singed and that the flesh on his pumped up arms was raw and slick.

A small dog yapped nearby and the palm leaves slapped in the breeze. Mel closed the window and pulled down the metal shutter. Then she cleaned her teeth, pissed and went to bed, where she lay, wide-eyed and tense, until two. Then she got up again and peeked through a gap in the blinds.

The courtyard was empty.

The next time she saw him was in daylight, on a cool January day with mist on the sea and drizzle in the air. The promenade was deserted – even the old fisherman who cooked sardines on sticks over fires on the beach hadn't bothered coming – so Rory stood out.

He wasn't moving, just waiting, as if he'd worked out her routine and found the perfect spot to intercept her, outside an Argentine steakhouse. It was where she usually stopped to look at the sea through a gap in the commercial clutter on the beach.

She slowed for a moment until deeply-ingrained training kicked in: never back down, never show you're scared, no daughter of mine... She set her face in a stiff smile and began to move with purpose, just short of swagger.

A few feet away, exactly where she would have stopped if Rory had really been there, head and all, she planted herself and gave a jerk of her chin in greeting.

'I asked you before – what the fuck. Do. You. Want?'

There was a smell about him, she realised, like burnt toast and roast beef.

He lifted his arm and pointed with a raw, baby-fat finger. It was such a real, human gesture, exactly Rory. She shivered and followed the line of his finger which led her eye to a brutalist block, the Hotel Salobreña Deluxe, with its row of faded, flapping European flags.

She heard footsteps and glanced over her shoulder. An elderly German couple she'd seen around town passed with their poodle. The man, white-haired and wearing a hunting jacket, gave a brief nod. His wife pursed her lips in disapproval. Either they couldn't see Rory or were too polite to mention the charred, headless monster in Adidas tracksuit bottoms.

Rory lowered his hand.

'What? Should I go there?'

In lieu of a head to shake, Rory waved a red hand from side to side.

Mel looked again at the hotel. There were lights on and cars parked outside. Guests. People from out of town. She was sure nobody knew about the flat she'd bought here – certain.

When she looked back, Rory had gone.

That night, Mel made sure the gun was loaded and handy on her bedside table, and before she fell asleep she resolved to change her routine.

She was at the supermarket when they caught up with her. However hard she tried, she couldn't do without English teabags and it was the only place that sold them. She always went on Wednesday afternoon.

They were waiting for her in the car park, sitting on the bonnet of the Honda. One she recognised – tall, bald and pickled in lager over the course of four decades – though she didn't know his name. The other was Wayne, a bouncer at one of Aidan's clubs, more fat than muscle these days. They were both dressed in generic cargo shorts and pastel shirts, with Ben Sherman deck shoes.

'Alright, Mel,' said Wayne. 'Long time no see.'

'Alright, Mel,' said the other man – a Glaswegian, it turned out. 'We've not met. I'm Ricky.'

Wayne glanced sideways and Mel put into words what she knew he was thinking – what she'd have been thinking if Aidan had given her this job.

'It's in your interest not to go around introducing yourself to people you're about to try to bump off, Ricky, you daft jock cunt,' she said.

Wayne laughed. He knew what she was doing, trying to rile Ricky so he'd get get overheated and do something stupid, giving her a chance to bolt.

'You ain't changed,' he said. 'We're parked over there. Give you a lift?'

He pointed to a rented BMW.

Rory was sitting in the back seat.

'He with you, then?'

This did throw Wayne. He squinted and pulled back his upper lip to reveal nicotine-stained teeth.

'You what?'

'That big headless bastard in the car. Rory.'

Ricky sucked his teeth and winced and looked at Wayne.

'She's cracked.'

'She's out of order,' said Wayne. 'He was only a kid, Mel. His mother couldn't see the body. I went to his confirmation. It ain't funny. Get in the car.'

Mel wished she'd brought the gun but you didn't, did you, when you were popping out for P.G. Tips and H.P. Sauce? She slipped in next to Rory and again noticed his barbecue stink. Better, she supposed, than that deodorant he used to wear.

Ricky drove, elbow out of the window, cigarette in his mouth. Wayne sat hunched and uncomfortable, wheezing and wet despite the winter cool.

'What's the plan then, lads? You could have just done me back there, pop pop, off you go.'

'Aidan wants to talk to you first,' said Wayne.

'He's here?'

'Nah. Zoom.'

Mel looked at Rory and for a moment doubted herself. He wasn't moving. No hand gestures this time. Was it possible they'd actually dug him up and propped his corpse in the seat?

They were driving out of town into the desert, past the vast salad sheds and fruit fields when Wayne pointed at a roadside petrol station.

Blow Up

'Pull in here, Rick. Need to top up if we're going to get to... If we're, uh, going to get there tonight.'

As Ricky came off the road, Wayne fiddled with the locking system to make sure the back doors couldn't be opened from inside. The car stopped and Wayne got out. Ricky put the radio on and tapped his fingers to a pop tune from the late Franco era, making the cigarette bob in his mouth. Mel shivered and looked across to where Rory had been.

He was gone – no, he was on the forecourt, following Wayne around the car. The locks hadn't stopped him. It was the first time she'd seen this new Rory walk and it hardly seemed strange. It was the gait she knew and the lack of a head hadn't made him any less cocky. Wayne was trying to work out the pumps and had the dripping dispenser in his hand. Rory kept moving towards Wayne and then something happened Mel couldn't parse – a moment of heat haze before Wayne fell to the floor grasping at his chest.

'Oh, for fuck's sake, fat fucking bastard,' said Ricky, shaking loose ash as he spoke. He jumped out of the driver's seat and scrambled around the long bonnet of the car.

Rory was now in front of the car pointing through the windscreen at the steering wheel. Mel understood immediately and scrambled over, sliding into position and reaching for the keys Ricky had left dangling. She bolted the doors, started the engine and reversed away, as confident behind the wheel of a car as ever.

As Wayne lay flat out, Ricky began to panic. His cigarette dropped. He drew a gun from the back of his shorts and waved it in the direction of the fast receding BMW. Mel spun it and slipped through the gears as she accelerated away towards the misty red mountains on the horizon.

In the rear view mirror, she saw Rory raise his arms.

Flames rose, then came a roar, a globe of white light, black smoke and alarms. Mel felt a hot wind rush by and, for a moment, smelled body-spray and sweat.

Red Hill

The car labours up the snow-covered road. You ride the accelerator and the brakes. The high pines on either side shed silver dust and show black against a cloudy sky slipping from grey to blue. Then, as the road curves, a warm glow – the neon sign of a small diner, a box in prefabricated aluminium. What does the sign say? It isn't clear, even when you squint. If you can just...

The car labours up the snow-covered road. You ride the accelerator and the brakes as it slips and resists. The car's heater exhales warm, dusty air from a slot on the dash. The high pines on either side shed silver dust, quiver with the weight of snow on their branches, and show black and razor-backed against a cloudy sky slipping from winter grey to night-time blue. Then, beyond the curve of the road, a glimpse of red – the warm glow of the neon sign of a small diner, a box in prefabricated aluminium. The sign says RED HILL DINER. Just a hundred more yards. Almost there.

The car labours up the snow-covered road. You ride the accelerator and the brakes. The car's heater exhales dusty air. The pines shed silver, and quiver. They show black against the winter dusk. Then, beyond the curve, a red neon sign: RED HILL DINER. Just a hundred more yards, if the car will allow it. Come on, baby, come on. Off the road, into the small parking lot, salted and snowless. Park between two pickups, neither old but both well-used. Switch off the engine, kill the heater, feel the cold at once.

The car labours up the snow-covered road between black pines until, beyond the curve, you see the red neon sign of the Red Hill Diner, two pick-ups in its parking lot and windows bright. You coax the car into the parking lot and switch off the engine.

Municipal Gothic

The heater dies. The cold begins to bite. You sit for a moment, looking out, beyond the faded red flank of the Ford truck to the yellow light of the diner window and the hot sizzle of the sign. Gloves on, hat on – time to leave the safety of the car and go inside, eat something, drink some coffee.

The car labours up the snow-covered road between the pines, towards the neon of the Red Hill Diner. You coax the car into the lot and kill the engine. You sit in the cold for a moment, looking at the light from the diner, before putting on gloves and your hat and opening the car door. It's only a few steps to the door and as you get near, the sound of country music drifts on the air. You reach for the handle.

The car labours between pines, drawn towards the neon light of the Red Hill Diner and the promise of hot coffee and fatty food. Into the lot, kill the engine, gloves, hat, and out. Just a few steps in the cold to the door. You reach for the handle and pull. A bell rings as you enter. The lights are off, suddenly, and nobody is here. A voice on the radio sings 'The Sounds of Goodbye'. You wait for a moment, listening, watching the shadows for movement. Everything abrades.

Up the hill between the pines, as fast as the car will go in the snow, desperate to reach the neon sign of the Red Hill Diner and drink a cup of hot coffee. Into the lot. The car radio is playing 'The Sounds of Goodbye' and you leave the engine running so you can listen to the final verse and the sob in Vern Gosdin's voice as he realises his wife is leaving for good. The song ends, a jingle begins, you kill the engine. The cold hits at once. You glance towards the door of the diner and its warm light.

Red Hill

The car struggles along Red Hill Road as it curves towards the sign of the Red Hill Diner, beneath tall pines, covered with snow that looks blue in the twilight. You park between two Ford pick-ups and don't hesitate – you need a cup of coffee and something to eat, and it's cold in the car. You slam the car door, lock it, and dash across the salted asphalt which crunches beneath your leather soled boots. You grab the handle and enter. A bell rings as you slip into the heat and light. The smell of coffee grounds drying on the griddle gives the air a black tang. On the radio, 'The Sounds of Goodbye'. There is a woman behind the counter. She has dirty-blonde hair and a blue uniform that needs pressing. She opens her mouth to speak but no sound comes. Space distorts.

Red Hill Road seems to go on forever. You push the car over the snow, riding the brakes and accelerator. Every now and then, the tires fail to bite and the car slips backward. Your hands, in the leather gloves Sherry bought you the Christmas before she left, grip the wheel too tight. You need a break – you need a coffee and something to eat. As if you've summoned it with that thought, you see a glow ahead beneath the black pines with their silvered branches: a diner in an aluminium box with a neon sign. Just a hundred yards more and then, under a blueing sky, you glide onto the salted parking lot and take a spot between two Ford pickup trucks, one blue, one faded red. You kill the engine and brace yourself for the cold. It's only a couple of steps to the door but you know it's going to bite. After a moment, like somebody jumping into the frozen sea, you launch yourself out of the car, slam the door, and head for the entrance. A bell rings when you enter and you hear country music, smell burning coffee grounds, and see a woman who looks a little like Sherry at the same age. Before you can utter a greeting she says, in a quivering whisper, 'Go! Get help. Get. Help.' But you can't – you can't move.

You sit in the car with the engine off. Your hands are on the wheel, warm in the leather gloves Sherry bought you before she left, and the neon light of the diner bathes you in red. The Red Hill Diner, Red Hill Road, Davisburg – you've been here before, though you can't remember when. Perhaps you drove through this way back in '76 when head office was pushing those new livestock insurance policies. You need a coffee but you're too tired to move and you know it will be even colder outside the car. You sigh. You make a move. A few steps across the salt-strewn asphalt, up two steps, and in through the door of the aluminium box. A bell rings. Vern Gosdin sings from a radio, about silence, and pain, and the tears of a grown man. The waitress behind the counter looks afraid. Her eyes lead yours to the floor: at the end of the counter, a pair of legs and feet in heavy work boots. A shadow moves across the back wall – someone is coming from the kitchen, whistling along with the music on the radio: '...a violent rush of teardrops from my eyes...' Somehow, his very tread is mean.

The car labours up the snow-covered road beneath dark pines that disappear into mist. Night is falling and the world is turning blue. You see a neon sign up ahead – Red Hill Diner. You could really use a cup of coffee, you've been driving in this god awful weather all day, but as you draw near, something tells you not to stop. As you pass, the car floating soundlessly, now, you watch shadows move beyond the condensation on the window – slow, submerged ghosts. People you will never know.

Imp Adrift

I was summoned into being when London was called Londinium, in a temple without corners, awash with sacrificial gore. I served many in the centuries that followed. My stench befouled palaces and great houses. I was nourished on nothing but blood and milk from the bodies of those I served, sucking at teats those wretches grew with the selling of their souls. I became fat as they grew weak. But, alas, I no longer so easily feast on star stuff. I must scrape scraps from the bones of chickens left in the gutters. I gnaw on stale bread from black sacks left in alleyways and yards. I pick through compost for morsels of green meat, like a rat. I am ashamed to find myself masterless and hungry in this low place.

What am I? If you beheld me, what would you see?

Some of my kind resemble cats, dogs or other such beasts that are welcomed at man's hearth. Others take the form of rodents, less welcome but not unearthly. But I? I would seem to be a unique creation. I understand myself to be disgusting to look upon. Perhaps I was distorted in the act of summoning, twisted in the journey between moons, or given the shape of a creature not of this world for some reason beyond my knowing. I am small. I have grey fur. I run on four raw, red feet that resemble scalded human hands. My eyes are black, except when the moon catches them, when they shine green. My lips are the colour of fresh bruises and my long tongue is midnight blue, like a hanged man's.

My appearance matters little, however, because I am rarely seen, though you may have heard me. On a summer night when you leave your window open and something shakes your garden hedge, or in winter when scratching in the attic wakes you, it may be me. I have no home, but from time to time I visit or invade. I never settle, however, because I must always hunt for a new master or mistress. It is my purpose. When there were fewer people and belief was stronger, I was never without. Now, even with so many bodies, the intervals grow longer. It has been thirty years since last I latched my teeth onto a warm one.

Lately, faintly, my hope has grown: I have the scent.

The noise and interference of millions of people makes the signal hard to set fast upon but I detect it and, like a hound after a crippled bird, I circle and track, drawing nearer each day.

It is a woman, which was always my preference, when preference I could afford to hold. I cannot say why. I had no mother, being created whole and perfect like Adam, and the only lust I feel is for blood, milk and chaos. I remember well a mistress, Hannah Wiley of Tewkesbury, who stroked me and oftentimes held me in her arms as she slept, too mad and too foul-smelling herself to mind my stink. Perhaps this fixed in my mind an idea of the tenderness of woman, even though I watched her strip a child of its skin and though I supplied her from my very flesh the poison she fed to her own newborn daughter.

In this new prospect, in the constant, silent cry she emits, unconsciously, like a beacon, I sense all the necessary feeling. She suffers isolation, hatred, yearning, fragile sanity. These are notes to which I am especially attuned. They pull me as a magnet pulls iron. For more than fifty days I have made my eccentric circuits, running on twisted legs in drains and ditches.

And now, at last, I see her with my own eyes.

This place is a kind of purgatory, neither town nor country. It is paved fine but lonely, wind-haunted. The buildings have no windows, only iron boxes that blow out hot air, roaring into the night. There are lights brighter than any Rome ever knew but they are cold, fixing the world in blood-stealing white. They bear names: Argos, Kuehne Nagel, John Lewis, Amazon.

She, my She, sits behind one of the buildings, upon a ledge, beneath a shelter that stops the rain but not the midnight frost. She smokes tobacco weed and looks into the light of a telephone held in a glovéd hand. She is grey and weary, thin and shivering.

My fur is wet and befouled. My eyes are dark. I breathe like a thing already dead, though die I cannot and never shall. I run beneath the fence, across white lines and yellow ones. I stop beyond the circle of the light. From those dark shadows, I call to her in my warmest, most especially enchanting voice. I put into it all my powers of weird music, purring like a poet in love.

'Just one drop of your sweet blood for me to drink, madam, and renounce God, and I shall bring you anything you may desire that may be found upon the earth, or in heaven.'

At the sound of the first word, she drops the device and the cigarette. One shatters and dies in starlight. The other bounces and sparks red. But there is no cry, no flight. She stares into the blackness and waits. She is enthralled.

I smell the air.

What does she want?

What does she need?

What has she lost?

With a great expenditure of vital energy, of which my supply is already short, I am able to penetrate and feel among the shallow tide of her mind. Pain, joy, pictures, names… Yes, there is the key, I have it.

'I will bring your child to you. I will find…' I test my gift to its fullest. 'Chiara.'

She steps forward. Will she take my bait, or spit at me?

'How do you know about Chiara?'

She sees not my ugliness. She is entranced, my magic acting upon her like hashish or opium. I have her.

'Do you renounce God?'

'God? I don't... Whatever, yes,' she whispers. 'Blood, you said, didn't you?'

I have chosen well. She understands at once this new reality and does not question my being or my offer. I come further from my hiding place and run to her on my ever-painful rotten paws. She smiles. I wonder what she sees in her enchantment. Her eyes glint beneath lowered lids. I bound, mount her, climb, burrow and – oh, delicious moment! – bite. Her flesh is warm and perfumed with sweat. The only sound she makes is a most blissful sigh. Her blood is thin stuff and sour, which is the way with the old ones, but with each drop, I bloom. I emerge from beneath her garments foul, fat and content.

'Lindsay, love – you're late off your break.'

I climb to Mistress Lindsay's shoulder and hiss. I whisper.

'Would you have me silence him? Bite him? Blind him? Burst his heart in his chest? I am your servant. Anything you wish.'

'I'm on my way,' she shouts. 'Dropped my phone. Sorry. Won't be a minute.'

A door closes and we are once again alone.

'What's your name?'

'I am called Robin Ripple, or the Childe Ripple, or Rip, but you may name me as you wish, just as you may command me.'

'I need to go back to work.' She points. 'Can you wait for me? I finish at three.'

'Three hours, three days, or three hundred years, I stand at your service always.'

'Three hours is fine.'

Imp Adrift

She lives on the edge of a moor where the trees bend sideways and sirens sound after midnight. Her house is bare with one chair, a table and walls black with mould.

'I've nothing,' she says, staring into an empty cupboard.

'Tell me, what would you eat?' I ask from the darkness of my nest beneath the table.

'What do you mean?'

I spend some of my newfound energy and summon a pork chop with butter and potatoes on a blue china plate, after one I saw upon the Duke of Wharton's table.

'No.'

I replace it with a loaf and a fine Stilton cheese alive with maggots.

'Just toast.'

Two slices are called into being. A chair scrapes. She chews. I crawl from my nest and curl at her feet, lapping softly at her toes with my blue tongue.

'About Chiara.'

'Yes, yes, I will bring her to you.'

'How, though? She's... You know... Gone.'

'For me, there is no "gone". There is no here, no there, no then, no now. It is all as one.'

She chews like a cow in the field.

'Now? Can you do it here, in daylight? Do we need to be at a cemetery at midnight or something?'

'There is no day, no night. Yes, now, of course, if you wish it.' I press my teeth against the flesh of her foot, break the skin as softly as if it were that of a grape. 'I must feed first.'

The child is no more difficult to summon than the pork chop, only being a greater volume of meat. She appears whole, pink in her cheek, lively of eye. Only her garments speak of the grave, soiled and half-rotten.

Mistress Lindsay is overcome. Rushing across the empty room she leaves bloody prints on the carpet. She takes the child in her arms.

'Mum?' says the child. 'Where are we?'

'It's my new house,' says Lindsay. 'I moved here after you– Oh, love!'

'I'm cold.' She looks about her. 'Where's Daddy?'

'Daddy went away.'

'After I… After the…'

From my hiding place, I see the child frown.

'I was walking to school, wasn't I?

'Come and sit with me at the table,' says Lindsay. 'Eat some breakfast. I'll get you a jumper or something.'

Chiara's hand fits into Lindsay's.

Cramp assails me. The effort is great.

They take two steps together in silence.

The bridge will not hold. I become muddled and hazy.

'Mummy, I–'

The child ceases to be. Mistress Lindsay's hand twitches, grasping at air.

After she has cried, and slept, and drunk – after I have crept into her bed and fed – after she has slept, and cried and drunk again, she summons me. Rain blows across the moor rattles upon the black window panes. She blows smoke.

'Will I be with her again? Afterwards, I mean.'

I lick my fur, bury my eyes beneath a stinking paw.

'There is no afterwards, there is–'

'Talk fucking sense, will you?'

Her shout is louder than the gale.

'It is a matter of souls,' I whisper. 'There are planes and categories… I cannot explain. Would you have me summon her again? I am stronger now.'

Lindsay extinguishes the cigarette and wipes her nose on the sleeve of her dressing gown. She shakes her head.

She rests her head on her arm and sleeps.

We shall be content, this woman and I. How many years until she is drained, I cannot say, but this is, at least, a safer age for witches and their familiars.

Protected by Occupation

I'm lying on the sofa at a friend's house, in the dark, worrying about where I'm going to sleep tomorrow, when my phone rings.

'Charlie boy,' says a grit-chewing smoker's voice on the line.

'Uncle Bernard?'

'That's my name, don't wear it out. Where are you?'

'In bed,' I whisper, not wanting to disturb my reluctant hosts in the room along the hall.

'Still looking for work?'

'How did you get this number?'

'Do you want a job or not? I heard you were embarrassing the family, asking for handouts left right and centre.'

'I've got a job.'

It is true. I've been working behind the bar of a pub in the city centre, taking the shifts nobody else wants, and washing dishes the rest of the time.

'I've got a better one for you. How do you fancy sitting on your arse, rent free, for six months?'

'Was it Phil? Did Phil give you the number?'

There is silence then the phlegmy rattle of his breath against his badly-fitting false teeth.

'Have you seen the news about my latest development down at Stoke Barton?'

'No.'

'Got the money boys frothing, it has – brownfield, derelict property, up-and-coming area. Planning permission for four hundred flats. My biggest yet. Know the area?'

'No.'

In fact, I don't even know where Stoke Barton is, though I've seen the name on the fronts of buses and on road-signs. I have a feeling it's somewhere under the motorway where the graffiti is dense and the street-lights flicker.

'Fuck me, you don't know much, do you?'

I sit up. I rub a hand through my thinning hair then over my dry eyelids.

'What derelict property?'

'Well, now, that's the interesting bit... Heard of the Red House?'

'Yes, I think so,' I say, uncertain.

'Hibberton House is its proper name but nobody's called that in years. Listed, it is. Tudor or something.'

I hear a creak and the click of a light switch elsewhere in the flat.

'I'm after a caretaker but it has to be someone I can trust. Someone to live on site. Keep the lights burning. Keep an eye on the damp. Chase the scrotes off.'

'I thought you said it was derelict?'

'I've had my boys fix up a nice little flat. Nicer than where you are now, I bet.'

'Bernard, I need to go, it's late, but–'

'Come and see me tomorrow, then, eh? At the Red House. Google it. Ten o'clock.'

I agree, not sure if I really intend to go, just to get him off the line, and hang up.

The door along the hall opens a crack. A white line, a silhouette and a growl.

'Charlie? Mate, it's nearly midnight, Jen and I both have work tomorrow.'

'Sorry, sorry,' I say, stammering and pathetic. 'I won't... I'm sorry'

There is a long silence before the door closes and I find myself in total darkness.

When I first see the Red House, it is two hundred metres away behind a fence topped with barbed wire, adrift in a maelstrom of brambles, and yet still somehow proud. I stand with my rucksack on my back, everything I own crammed into twenty-five litres of space, and stare, as the house stares back at me. I understand, now, how it got its name: the brick has a particularly vivid shade, insistent against the grey of the day.

Like the cloud from a detonation, a hundred or more pigeons burst from it in a chattering mass, out of the roof and through blank, paneless windows.

The sound that disturbed them comes to me a moment later. I turn to see a lime green van labouring up the unadopted, potholed lane. It pulls up and I read the motto on its flank: 'Brabart Properties Ltd – funky living spaces for striving professionals'.

Bernard struggles out of the driver's seat in a cloud of cigarette smoke.

He is wearing a cheap, oversized suit in a cut not fashionable for twenty years. Rings gleam, trapped below his knuckles. He rolls towards me, gut first, beaming.

'Charlie boy!'

A hand on my arm, those fat digits digging into the flesh, grinding bacon grease into my bones.

'I've missed seeing you.'

'Hello, Uncle Bernard.'

His hand drops away and he looks me up and down.

'You look like shit,' he says.

He slaps flat-footedly towards the temporary steel gate with its warning signs and chains and opens the padlocks one by one. Together, we drag the gate across rough concrete, scratching a white semi-circle.

Bernard draws on his cigarette and puffs a blue mist around his unruly head as he considers the overgrown driveway.

'Got decent boots on? Let's walk.'

I look down at my well-worn, thin-soled Adidas trainers, and follow.

'It's a lot of land,' I say, partly to break the uncomfortable rhythm of our synchronised steps.

Amid the brambles are the remains of concrete and brick structures, pieces of pipe cut off a few inches above ground, and chunks of rusting machinery. There are burst bags of rubbish, hurled over the fence and left for rats and gulls to tear apart. A lone boot grows moss.

'Lovely, isn't it?'

He isn't being sarcastic. To Bernard, it really does look beautiful, like a virgin plain beyond the frontier.

'They built parts for planes here before the War, until they moved production under Salisbury Plain. Offices in the house.'

The building is getting nearer, flooding the horizon red.

'Then it was billets for Italian prisoners of war, working on the farms.'

Beneath our feet, concrete gives way to relatively smooth asphalt and Bernard begins fingering his keys. We stop at the doorway with its clamshell hood and four white stone steps. Bernard struggles with the lock muttering to himself.

'Fucking thing... Checked it before I left the office... Should have... Fuck sake...'

I can hear the motorway in the distance, a constant exhalation, and the wind shaking the trees. There is also something else – a high, secret sound.

A signal.

From the moment I put a foot inside, I'm possessed by the Red House.

Altogether, it is grim – dusty in that way that almost amounts to topsoil, and thick in places with pigeon shit, rat shit, and drifts of dessicated insect carcasses. The air is heavy with spores and the musk of mice.

The entrance hall isn't grand, only a little larger than you'd find in any substantial suburban house. Most of it is taken up with a wide staircase. The corridor remaining at the side is correspondingly narrow. There is a large, plain table, mid-twentieth-century institutional, scattered with paperwork.

And there are murals, covering the plastered walls from ground to ceiling, all the way up the stairwell.

'Something, those, ain't they?' says Bernard, bustling past me, jingling his keys.

There is too much to take in.

Regimental banners: swags of red silk rendered in faded paint, with cleverly suggested gold crowns and royal blue ribbons. Classical scenes: the seven hills of Rome, the Antonine Gate and the Colosseum, an orgy with grapes, masks, naked flesh. Trompe l'oeil: marble statues in their own alcoves, windows looking out over gardens of olive trees, a sense of space implied through shade and highlights.

There are women, too. There is a line-up of blondes on one wall, naked and coquettish. On another surface, a reclining brunette in silk and heeled slippers, her hair set in a permanent wave, smoke from a cigarette holder tickling around her to form spectral groping hands, her pubic hair lovingly detailed.

'Eyetie prisoners did them,' says Bernard. 'And that's just one problem I've got, Charlie boy. These paintings are ugly as hell but they're listed. Can you believe that? I can't demolish the building. Okay, fine, I can work around that – but you're telling me I can't get rid of this shit? Who the hell wants to live in a luxury flat with this lot on the walls?'

I am mesmerised.

'Me.'

Bernard tuts.

'Oh, yeah? You ain't seen the best one yet.'

He leads me further into the building, to a room big enough to play a game of tennis. Shards of plasterboard snap beneath my feet. It is dark because of the ragged blackout curtains covering the windows so Bernard snaps on his torch.

'Jesus Christ,' I say, thrown off balance.

The entire wall is covered with a single image. It is a child's face, a parody of an innocent cherub, blue-eyed and red-cheeked, like something from a Victorian soap advertisement.

'This is my other problem,' says Bernard. 'The Angel of the Red House, they call it. One of the eyeties painted this, too.'

'Who is she?'

Bernard growls.

'Who knows? Who cares? She ain't nobody.'

He looks at me, hands stuffed into the lined pockets of his sheepskin coat, and chews his own false teeth in defensive consternation.

'Upstairs,' he says after a moment, and gestures with fat fingers.

The staircase feels flimsy, each step wobbling in its setting, and I think I see something scurry away as I reach the first landing.

'I heard you split up with that girl you were with,' says Bernard, wheezing behind me. 'What was her name? Melinda? Belinda?'

'Beth.'

'Yeah, that's it.'

We reach the upper floor. All the doors are closed and it is dark but for stripes of white light where their frames have warped. Bernard feels around the walls searching out switches.

'I always thought you could do better, personally,' he says through grunts of exertion. 'She was alright as a training exercise and all that, but hardly–'

'Uncle Bernard, please.'

There is a click and the lights come on, slowly – ten or so incandescent bulbs arranged in an ugly chandelier.

'Ah, there we go.'

There are no more paintings or murals up here, just blankness in a corridor whose walls are oddly too close together, along with scraps of old maps and notices.

Bernard moves suddenly.

I look where his head has turned, towards the still black end of the hall where the dim light doesn't reach.

There is a distant sound, like bone on bone.

Bernard directs his torch into the gloom and the scratching stops.

There is nothing there, though the air seems live.

Bernard laughs unconvincingly, rubs at his big blackhead-covered nose with two thick fingers, and switches off the torch.

'Here's your apartment.'

He pushes open a door and daylight floods out.

The room has been patched and painted plain white. It smells of emulsion and freshly-cut wood. There is a simple double bed with a white frame, made up with white bedding; an old wooden dining chair; a well-worn antique desk; and a TV on a stand. There is also a simple kitchen with a hot-plate, microwave, kettle and sink. A box of groceries sits on the desk.

'Very nice,' I say.

'Well, don't sound so surprised. Electrics are a bit dodgy so don't boil the kettle and cook at the same time. You'll need to go to a laundrette to do your washing. There's a shower on the ground floor – grotty, but it works.'

He hands me his keys.

'I'll run you through all this lot and then leave you to it. And remember, the main thing is – all you need to do – is live here, keep the lights burning, let people see you coming and going. Most of these scrotes…' He waves a hand to indicate the whole world. 'They like to think they're brave but they're chickens if they think there's any chance of being chased off.'

I weigh the keys in my hand.

'Why not just hire a proper security firm? Why me?'

'I told you,' he begins, an uncharacteristic note of uncertainty in his voice.

'You didn't tell me. You said you were *going* to tell me.'

'Well, it's just easier if it's family, isn't it?'

'And I'm cheap, I suppose.'

'Charlie!' he says, putting a hand to his supposedly broken heart.

Have you ever felt alone? Really, really alone? Even when you're on your own at home, you can hear the neighbours pottering about, putting the kettle on, flushing the bog at two in the morning, watching *Antiques Roadshow*. At the Red House, I can see for a quarter of a mile in every direction – car showrooms by the river, factory sheds, cement silos, cranes, and seagulls over the landfill site. The rooms above me are empty. The basement is empty. Any room I'm not in – empty. If I cough, it echoes like a gunshot in a canyon.

At first, I turn on every light and leave them on. It doesn't help much. Incandescent bulbs, 40 watt at best, barely make a dent on the darkness in that upstairs hallway. And, worse, with the lights on, the windows become mirrors. I can't see out but anyone outside on the wasteland – vandals, thieves, fly-tippers, junkies – could see in. But that's the point, I suppose: I'm on display.

I check all the locks, drag a chest of drawers across the inside of the front door to be on the safe side, and retreat towards my little apartment, turning off lights as I go.

It is alright up there – it really is. Better than anywhere I've lived in a long time. I just have to tell myself it is a normal room in a normal house on a normal street and I feel fine for, oh, minutes at a stretch.

There's a sensation that's hard to describe, though, where you know – you just know – someone is on the other side of a door, listening and breathing as lightly as they can, but close. And I just cannot shake it.

I put the telly on but after twenty minutes I start to worry that the chatter will stop me hearing sounds from the hallway, so I turn it off.

My eyes keep drifting to the gap at the bottom of the door. Is there a shadow there? Someone moving outside? The harder I stare, the noisier the signal seems to get.

I turn off the lamp at the bedside and hold my breath in the darkness.

The house creaks. I shiver. The shadows on the ceiling shift as a car passes on the main road and I am glad for the momentary connection with another human being, however remote.

If there is anyone else there they are holding their breath, too. In fact, yes, I am sure I can hear somebody not breathing – focusing on me, directing all their mental energy in my direction.

'Fuck sake, this is ridiculous,' I say explosively, trying to break the spell.

Somewhere nearby, too nearby to make sense, a cat meows as if in response.

I try to sleep.

When day comes its light is cool and dilute. I need the toilet which means I need, first, to confront the cold air of the room and, next, to make my way down the dark corridor to the bathroom along the hall. Institutional green paint peels from the walls and the bathtub is full of brick dust. Water drips from the cistern. The mirrors are foxed and turning black at the edges. I piss, wash my hands in cold water and then stop to stare at myself. I look like shit. Old and worn thin.

I step back out into the hall with its persistent sighing draught and hurry back to my sanctuary. I get dressed, make coffee and decide that, if I'm the caretaker, I ought to patrol the property. Perhaps if I know it better, I'll sleep better, too. It is, after all, only a building.

Bernard has left a rechargeable builder's torch spattered with white paint. From my own rucksack I take a notebook and pencil so I can draw a map. My phone will do for a camera. For a moment I feel as if I know what I'm doing. Then an unkind laugh escapes – I'm like a child playing at being an explorer. It's ridiculous. But I go on with the job.

The Red House has four storeys. There are attic rooms originally intended for servants and a large basement. What I'd seen by the dim light of the previous evening hadn't left much of an impression beyond darkness and dirt. Now, with daylight creeping in through various openings and filthy window panes, the picture is clearer. It feels like a school or borstal. Every room is painted the same combination of custard yellow and milk chocolate brown. What furniture remains is of austerity-grade plywood. There are desks, tables, cheap stacking chairs. There are notice boards all over the place with rectangles faded into the felt. Corners and strips of paper remain: 'Ministry of Supply Notice 147D – use of timber for non-essential purposes'; 'Ministry of War Notice 982(b) – blackout enforcement'; 'Entertainments committee – would you like to learn how to build model ships from matchsticks? *Ti piacerebbe imparare a costruire modellini di navi?*'

The basement has a kitchen and canteen. There is a warped wooden counter and a tarnished tea urn. Tables are scattered about and shards of broken crockery cover the floor. The kitchen looks old with a rusting range and a vast stone basin. There is nothing in the pantry but rat shit and two empty quart-sized bottles that once held George's Bristol Stout. The shelves are lined with yellow sheets from an 80-year-old edition of the *Evening Post*.

I've already seen the main rooms of the ground floor but towards the rear of the house there are a few smaller spaces. Offices, mostly, created with temporary partitions. I need the torch, here, because the windows have been broken and then boarded. Empty shelves. Desks askew. Ceiling tiles shattered on the floor. I squeak a rusty Anglepoise lamp back and forth, open and close some drawers. All I find is a copy of *Men Only* from 1948, its corners chewed by mice, and a few empty cigarette packets of a similar vintage, squashed flat.

Upstairs, apart from my room and the bathroom, the doors are locked. Bernard gave me a set of keys on a comically large loop. I try them one after the other until the first door pops open.

It is a dormitory with space for ten beds, nine of which are still in place – steel-framed military bunks. Otherwise, it has been stripped bare. It feels dry, dusty and dead. The other locked doors conceal a guardroom, with its own cot, telephone and a small desk, and a windowless walk-in cupboard, empty except for a shattered picture frame and a broken deckchair.

The final door leads to another dormitory, this time with three bunks remaining. The damp has got into this room, making the plaster bubble and blacken. Around the window, buddleia has invaded, pulling apart the bricks and blocking the light.

I realise I'm holding my breath and force myself to exhale.

I feel something here – an additional weight in the air, or a high-pitched whine just out of hearing.

Stepping across broken glass and plaster, through inch-thick dust, I approach the wall between two bunk beds. There are more drawings and some writing, but only faint, in pencil on bile-yellow paint.

I shine the torch on them.

It's the Angel again or at least a young girl with a similarly dreamy expression. This artist had real skill. Working in graphite on rough plaster, he captured the lightness of her cotton dress, the gleam in her eye, a look that suggests–

What's the writing? Italian, of course, and in the kind of cursive that makes old letters and documents hard enough to read at the best of times. *Verra… notte… cuore…* I find a translation app on my phone and point the camera at the text. After a few moments with the words dancing on screen, blinking in and out of existence, it suggests something: '…in the night. Guard your heart.'

I feel something slide around my ankle, softly stroking the bone.

I jolt backwards, shaking my leg in reactive, animal terror.

What was it? A rat?

No, of course not. I know exactly what it felt like.

I head to the nearest pub I can find, under a railway bridge by an industrial park, hoping that beer will relax me. It is called The Saracen Inn and looks almost as old as The Red House. Posters in the window say THIS IS A DRUG FREE PUB and ANTI-SOCIAL OR CRIMINAL BEHAVIOUR WILL NOT BE TOLERATED ON THESE PREMISES. Through frosted glass, the low light looks hospital green. I enter and hear the final bars of 'Jolene' by Dolly Parton. A woman in late middle-age is behind the bar – grey-haired, smoke cured, glasses on a chain.

'What can I get you, love?'

I order a pint of Carling.

The rolling opening riff of 'Jolene', apparently on repeat, comes from a speaker on the ceiling.

While the woman pulls the beer I glance at the only other customer. He is an elderly man with a copy of the *Times* and a bottle of Guinness Foreign Extra. His black skin seems to have taken on a layer of fine dust or ash. He looks up and jabs a grey finger at the newspaper.

'What they need to do, you see, is invest in infrastructure. Create jobs. Stimulate the economy. Old fashioned Keynesian economics. Right?'

'Leave him alone, Rodney,' says the woman behind the counter. 'Nobody cares. Nobody's interested.'

'Shut up, woman. I'm a paying customer, I deserve a little respect.'

'You're a pain in the arse. Four pounds ten, love.'

'Four. Pounds. Ten. Pence?' says Rodney slowly. 'You're a thief, too, woman. Son, check your change when she gives it to you. What's that? A ten pound note? Check your change.'

She tuts and rolls her eyes.

The pub has three rooms, or sections, all barren. One has a pool table with torn baize, another a carpet and the third bare boards and benches. An unusual impulse overtakes me and I say to Rodney: 'Mind if I join you?'

He looks startled, then pleased, though he tries to conceal it.

'Sure, no problem.'

'I've just moved into the area,' I say.

'Bloody gentrification,' he says.

I laugh, once, too loud.

'I'm the...' I can't think of the right word. 'Watchman, I suppose, at the Red House.'

Rodney looks at me over the upper rim of his glasses.

'What d'you say?'

'I'm living there. To protect it.'

He nods slowly and folds his paper.

'Now that's interesting. Been a loooong time empty.'

'The developer who bought it is going to build flats.' I didn't want to mention Bernard.

'Of course he is. All anybody wants – flats, flats and more flats. Rat holes.'

His hand goes to the beer bottle in front of him and he turns it round on the bar runner, smoothing its neck with his thumb.

'Do you know much about the building?' I ask. 'It seems old. I heard Tudor.'

'No, not that old. Seventeenth century.' He calls to the barmaid who has drifted into the back room. 'Fran! The Red House – what do you think, seventeenth century sound right?'

Fran ambles over.

'The Red House? That horrible old place. Yeah, something like that. The oldest building in the area, I heard. Why do you ask?'

Rodney jerks a thumb towards me.

'Boy's living there.'

Fran's eyebrows jolt upward involuntarily.

'Rather you than me, love.'

'Why do you say that?'

She wipes a cloth along the bar and straightens the charity boxes on the counter.

'Oh, just… I don't know. A bit lonely, innit? Cold, probably.'

Rodney clears his throat.

'When I was a kid in short trousers we used to run around the grounds.'

He rubs an arthritic finger through a deep crack in his cheek.

I take a sip of my beer.

'Soon stopped, though. Dangerous place to play.'

'All that rubble and metalwork.'

He rocks his head from side to side.

'Well, not so much that.'

He locks eyes with me.

'You see her yet?'

It feels at that moment as if someone is pulling out my spine in one long movement, filling the gap with cold metal.

'The mural, you mean? The "Angel of the Lodge"?'

Rodney puts the beer bottle to his lips and fills his mouth with beer. He chews it around, moving it from cheek to cheek to the pouch inside his lower lip. He swallows.

'That's her, yes.'

His watery eyes fix on me, watching for something in my expression or my body language. I smile.

'You can't miss the mural, can you? Bloody awful.'

He nods and waves a dismissive hand. There's something I haven't understood. He stands up with a groan and tucks in his shirt.

'Anyway, I'm here most days. Maybe see you again.'

With a lazy wave, he drifts towards the door and out into the street.

'Jolene' starts for the fourth time.

I grab the paper Rodney left behind and settle in for the evening.

Going back to the Red House is like arriving for my own execution. The darkness is deep away from the road, even with light pollution from the industrial estate and motorway. The cold feels more biting and the building itself is no longer red but black against the moon.

Singing seems the best approach, so I belt out 'Lazy Sunday' by the Small Faces for no particular reason other than that it feels as if shouting 'How's your Bert's lumbago?' into the deep blue might help.

Animals scatter in the dark but there's no sign of intruders. As I approach the door of the house, my singing drops in volume as if, subconsciously, I'm anxious about alerting it to my presence. With the key in my hand, in front of the lock, I stand in silence on the step and listen to my own breathing against the background rush of distant traffic. I sigh. I unlock the door and reach for the light switch. Kicking a chunk of plaster across the floor, I slam the door behind me.

'I'm home!' I shout, laughing.

The laugh is a lie I'm telling myself, but my body won't play along. There's cold sweat on my neck and my hands are shaking.

I look towards the dark doorways on either side of the staircase. I know I should check the place over before going to bed but I really don't want to.

'Come on, mate,' I say to myself. 'Don't be wet.'

Then I start laughing again, for real this time. Laughing at the stupid murals with their anatomically inaccurate tits and the very idea that my uncle – Uncle Bernard who eats two bacon butties a day and hasn't read a book since *Biggles and the Deep Blue Sea* – somehow owns a listed building.

I start my patrol, flicking on lights, shining the flashlight from my phone into dark corners and kicking open doors.

For a moment, for a couple of minutes, I feel pretty good, as if the spell has been broken. There is nobody there, nothing in the shadows, except mice and old newspapers. It's just a shitty old house. Miserable, yes, but not remarkable. As atmospheric, I tell myself, as a scout hut.

Then I get to the Angel.

She has changed.

That huge face, covering an entire wall, stares down at me with the same benign, bland beauty – totally innocent, or wanting me to believe so. Now, though, there are words. It is a simple phrase in what I suppose is black paint:

BRING ME A KITTEN

The house shifts around me.

Rodney is waiting for me and greets me with a shake of his pale palm.

'Fran, get the boy a pint of his usual.'

When I've climbed onto my stool at the bar, he slaps something down on the counter. A brown padded envelope.

'Had a look in my personal library after we spoke yesterday. Knew I had something.'

Fran places my pint. I thank her and ignore it.

Rodney opens the envelope and slides out a book. It's thin but smartly bound and bears the crest of Bristol University Press.

'Bought this from the cancelled book box at the library a few years ago. Always buy anything to do with local history.' He laughs. 'Don't always read 'em, though.'

I take the book from his outstretched hand. *Superstition and Ritual in Early Modern Somerset and Gloucestershire 1650-1730.*

'Chapter four,' says Rodney, raising his beer bottle in salute.

I open the book to a page marked with a yellow Post-It. The essay is called 'A new transcription of, and commentary on, the diary of Dr William Goodhind during 1714, and the Hibberton case'. The authors are two Americans. Flicking through the pages, I can see at once that the text is dense, in small type, with numerous even heavier footnotes.

'Hell of a story,' says Rodney. 'Take it with you.'

I close the book.

'Thanks, mate, yeah, I'll read that later.'

Fran wipes the bar around my elbow.

'You look exhausted,' she says.

'Didn't get much sleep.'

She and Rodney exchange a brief glance.

I drink a third of my pint in one go and wipe my mouth with my thumb.

'By the way, I don't suppose… Do either of you know where I could buy a cat?'

'A cat?' says Rodney, recoiling.

'I need a bit of company,' I say, managing a thin smile.

Fran sniffs.

'I think I know someone who knows someone.'

I approach the door of the Red House with a cardboard cat carrier under one arm, the book under the other, stepping woozily over the cracked concrete. I can feel the animal struggling. It whines and cries, then falls silent once the threshold is crossed. Submission.

Joking, I think, I call out loud: 'Got your kitten, darling.'

As I speak, the lights go out.

The cat hisses.

From the landing at the top of the stairs, in the deepest pit of shadow, I hear the distinct sound of a foot on a creaking board.

Have you ever shouted in a dream and woken yourself up only to hear yourself mumbling incoherently? I want to say, loud and clear, 'Who's there?' What comes out is a sort of dribble of noise. My throat closes up, my vocal cords refuse to resonate.

From the shadow, picked out by moonlight, a bare, dirty foot emerges, followed by a thin white ankle.

Time densifies, curves outward.

I see a wasted leg.

A swirl of dirty cotton.

I drop the book and the cat carrier. They fall in slow motion.

The box detonates. The animal bursts free, skitters along the hall.

There is a laugh which seems to come from the figure on the stairs.

It is a girl's laugh.

Simultaneously present and distant.

Bright and paper-thin.

I can see most of her, now – the nightdress filthy and spattered with black, the spindles of her fingers, the silhouette of a head held high.

Sincerely, desperately, I try to run.

My body is pumping the necessary chemicals but, at the same time, my muscles have seized.

I make another pathetic creaking sound around the petrified tongue that clogs my mouth.

One step at a time, as slow as if suspended in water, she moves down and down until, just as the cool blue light is about to reveal her face, she accelerates to a blur.

As she passes in front of me I feel flu shivers. Every bone cracks with pain.

But she doesn't want me.

From the hall with the mural of the Angel, I hear the cat howl, then silence, then that near-far laughter again, before the crunch and scrape of bone on bone.

15th November 1714
Returned from a visit upon my patient at Stapleton and fast abed when called upon by Dr Peacock in high agitation, soliciting my

assistance in a business at Stoke Barton which he would not describe but insisted on my seeing by my own eyes.

Ate a little beef and drank China tea, dressed against the frost, and went with him by his curate cart, and a little horse not fit for stew.

Found the child, Mary Monckton, at the parlour of the New Inn, in the care of her mother and father, adamant against returning to Hibberton House.

This house, an old one, was once the home of a gentleman now in London, maintained out of love for the memory of the family but rarely visited or used, and so under the care of Mr Monckton and his wife, who, though humble, live much as Lord and Lady, with their two daughters.

The room in which we gathered was poorly lit, mean and much bedevilled with vermin, which scratched and cried boldly throughout our interview, despite the stamping of my boot upon the boards.

Dr Peacock commanded Mary recount the events of that evening, and of the week fast gone. The child, who I should judge to be not beyond her thirteenth year, at first refused, but on being taken roughly by the arm by her father and shaken, submitted to tell the tale yet one more time.

(I later admonished the man, but did not do so in front of his wife and child, out of feeling for his position in the household.)

She stated that on the evening of 12th this month, soon after turning to her bed, she was awoken by a 'scratching echo' in the chamber, as if some beast or creature was present but beyond her sight.

Through this there was, she declared, a certain heaviness in the room. A disturbance of the ether as before a storm, I understood her to imply, or as during an eclipsing of the sun when birds do cease to sing.

When she cried vehemently the animal fell still a while, before then speaking.

I took particular note of the words she supposes to have heard there uttered but will not record them here. I rushed red in the face on hearing such language come from so bland a mouth, in so simple a Gloucestershire tongue. I seem to hear them yet now.

Yesterday, on the 13th, she heard the same scratching, and the voice once again spoke to her in vulgar terms.

Upon this instant, however, a form she could not see made assault upon her person. To which, she said, it seemed a mighty hand came about her face with such force that a bruise was there made. This she was able to exhibit – a yellow black-specked mark, and a swelling about the jaw.

This evening, 14th, the path was followed yet further. The beast came, made its foul ministration, laid its claw upon her, as before. Further, however, it dragged her from the bed, flung open the door, and hurled her entire person down the staircase into the hall.

She was, in evidence of this occurrence, able to point at certain marks upon the stair, and to bleeding beneath the skin of her back and flanks, which she showed me without shame, as might a creature of Eden.

Peacock was in no doubt of the truth of this account and pressed upon me to find fault in it. The parents were yet uncertain and so I enquired first of them: was the child a liar by habit? They believed not, pronouncing her both obedient, and a faithful sister to the younger child. Was she baptised, and strict in her prayers? At this I observed a slight coming together of the gazes, through such as which long-married people may convey great meaning. Insisting upon this, I withdrew an admission that she had not been baptised, and prayed but infrequently, despite much remonstrance.

Going on: had Mary lately come into her womanhood, or shown any sign of commencing the passage thereto? The girl protested but the mother answered freely: yes, the child had lately come that way. I drew no judgement but thought of certain like instances of domestic disturbance recorded in prior times, in Prussia, Holland and, I fancied, Worcester or some other such English town.

Continued. It being late, I thought against visiting Hibberton that night, but Peacock well argued that to see the house soon after the incident, and in the same condition of darkness, might tell much truth.

Taking a key from Mr Monckton, and a lantern from the inn, we walked the short way across a frost-bit common, and then into the grounds of the house.

I had not before laid eye upon Hibberton and saw little enough of it this night, for it was without moon or starlight. The lantern gave us the path and brought us to the door where I discerned a pronounced redness of the brick.

The storm-pricking Mary Monckton described was evident to me, and also to Peacock, who spoke hoarse and with a shiver in his voice. It seemed to me to be something between sense and sound, as a mighty waterfall is felt to vibrate in the rock before it is seen.

Peacock held the lantern while I fit the key to the lock and unbolted the door.

We neither pressed upon it being, frankly, afeared.

Peacock whispered, 'Do you not feel that something stands within, hard fast against the timber?'

I agreed that, indeed, I did.

Mastering myself, and wishing, I confess, to show myself a stronger man than Peacock, I pushed at the door. I felt resistance, I thought, though doubted myself at once, as it fell inward and we beheld a darkness beyond darkness, that the lamp could do naught against.

We neither of us entered but waited.

Then came a voice, saying clear, though as across a gulf.

'The child is mine and will follow my ways.'

Peacock, hearing same, dropped the lamp, which broke upon the earth. Its light expired and Peacock ran.

The door heaved shut with a most terrible firmness.

I undertook to follow my colleague in fleeing.

16th November 1714

Entreated Mr Monckton to bring Mary to my offices where in proper circumstance and with the best of the daylight I might examine the marks upon her body, and enquire further of her as to any instances at Hibberton.

She seeming drawn and shivering, with her father's permission, I offered her a glass of ale, warmed over the fire and sugared, which she held in both hands but did not taste.

'After your night at the inn, have you returned to the house?' I asked.

'Yes, sir. We slept there last night.'

'And what have you to report?'

Mr Monckton, looking toward the girl, begged her tell me.

'I believe, sir, that you know as well as do I,' said the precocious child, and a smile lighted upon on her face. Not a smile of innocence or of joy, but of knowing, and perhaps derision also, as if some other creature had momentarily peered through the portage of her delicate skull.

I took her to refer to the visit Peacock and I had made to the house, and our encounter there, and subsequent retreat.

Being students of natural philosophy, and rejecting superstition in all forms, we both had resolved that our hearing a voice, and feeling sure of a physical presence, was caused by temporary madness brought on in darkness.

Indeed, there are instances recorded of holy sisters and others so confined entering into a shared lunacy, and, though I look back upon my diary of but two days past, I find that I dispute my own memory.

I asked the girl once more and, seeming child again, she said that the scratching had once more been heard and that she had on this occasion been pulled from her bed, to the floor, and into the space beneath the bed.

Mr Monckton gave nodding assent to this account whereupon I begged him say more.

'Hearing her cry out, we found Mary neath the bed as she says, and pulling hard upon her hands, my wife and I were unable to bring her free.'

'Was any creature or person seen?'

'No, sir, but that such a thing was present, though invisible, I do not doubt one moment.'

He commenced to draw comparison with the act of the Moon upon the tides of the Earth, and of the weight of a fish at the end of a line.

Commanding her to remove her shawl I examined the upper arm where the assailant was supposed to have seized her, and then took to my knee to see the bruised ankle-bones where the hold was made during the struggle. There were indeed fingermarks, though indistinct, and larger I should say than could be made by most men. Certain scratches suggested the action of fingernails or animal claws.

I asked, 'Were words spoken?'

Mr Monckton avowed to have heard no such sound, nor even breathing or sighing as on prior visitations.

Mary said that some words were whispered before the assault.

'She asked me to bring a cat, or kitten.'

My ears pricked at this: first, arrested by 'she'; but also thinking of the incidence of witchcraft of older times, in which animal 'familiars' were so common a point.

'You agreed to do so?'

'I did, sir, and was then released.'

Her eyes cast over and a most delicate colouring came to her face.

'I must do as she asks, sir, or the punishment shall be worse at our next meeting.'

Curious, certainly, but also overcome with the desire to do a service by this charming child, I turned to her father and said, 'I should be glad to bring a cat for this purpose.'

Thereupon I rode to a farmer at St Anne's who I knew always to be in possession of a litter and acquired for two pennies a pair of creatures small enough to sit in the palm of my hand and as black as royal velvet. I know not why I chose black except that a feeling, remote but persistent, that she, *the creature, should be offended by ought else.*

Presenting the animals to the child, I laughed to see her pet and kiss them, forgetful in that instant of the circumstances of their procurement. She thanked me and took my hand to kiss it also which caused much embarrassment for my part and made me speak colder than I felt in compensation. She seemed wounded by my words.

This morning, word reached me that the girl had slept a sound night, though her parents had been much disturbed by sounds and movements throughout the house. The kittens, however, were found dead – their insides turned out, no less, upon the parlour hearth, and part burned.

18th November 1714

A dreadful day.

Slept but poorly, assailed by my own unquiet mind. In the foredrowsing, even, I thought of the girl, her eyes, the whiteness of her soft cheek and the plumpness about her middle. Then much troubled by dreams in which the child was present, addressed me most directly, calling me urgently to her embrace. As I approached, in this dream, she put forth arms red with gore from fingertip to the turn of each joint, as if into some butcher's basket she had reached. Awoke suddenly, sweating, thinking it had been no dream but a true vision.

Rising before dawn, I felt myself ill at ease by firelight until remembering how I did dream. Resolved then to visit the girl and to see her dainty hands myself, blood or no.

By cart at sunrise and reaching Hibberton Hall with sun and moon both astride the sky, my apprehension very great.

I found the door of the House ajar and darkness within. Calling from the step, I received no reply. I summoned myself and entered. I cast open the shutters of the hall at once, whereupon thin light did settle up on certain marks that stained the boards. Black marks, as I perceived them. Though cold fear gripped my very bones, I made passage through the house, shouting the names of Mary, Mr Monckton and his wife.

A foul odour, like that of the meat market in summer, overcame me as I climbed the staircase.

I found the family in the child's bedchamber.

Mr Monckton was in the same state as had been the kitten. That is to say, cut open and splayed. His wife also. And the younger child. All lay upon the bare floor, God save their souls. Mary, a child blessed with beauty but equally accursed, was upon the bed. In her small hand there was a blade. She had cut her own throat.

When I come round, there is complete silence. There is no presence, no weight in the air. The book is lying near my head, open, its pages fluttering in a draught. Then, bang – a single heavy knock sounds through the house. I scramble up from the ground and dust myself down. The knock comes again. It is the front door.

'Who's there?' I shout.

'It's me.'

Uncle Bernard. He sounds agitated. His voice is higher pitched and louder than usual. I keep him waiting for a moment then open the door. All round shoulders and skull, he charges in out of the rain.

'Are you alright?' he asks, wiping a hand through the stubble of his head and flicking the water away.

'Fine,' I say. I catch myself smirking, now. I am fine. I'm very well. I feel a certainty I haven't known in a long time.

Above us, steady, deliberate footsteps sound. Bernard's eyes bounce upward.

'What's that?' he asks.

'I don't know.'

He frowns.

'This is going to sound stupid but…' His face wrinkles. 'I had a dream about you.'

'A dream?'

I laugh. Bernard doesn't dream.

'I was worried about you.'

'I'm fine,' I say. 'But there's something I need to show you. Upstairs.'

I don't know where it came from but in my hand, there is a knife.

Director's Cut

Rod was a regular in The George. He had his own special pint glass and a place reserved at the bar. I knew he'd been an actor but didn't recognise him from any film I'd ever seen, and I've seen nearly every film ever made in Britain. That's my special area of expertise; I've written two books on it. Maybe he knew that. Maybe that's why, one Thursday night during the interval in the film quiz, when Wayne was playing his usual selection of Barry Gray TV themes, Rod spoke to me.

'Like films, do you?' His voice was wet and his breath smelled of lager.

'Sorry?'

'Like films? Your, er, whatsit. T-Shirt.'

I looked down. I was wearing a tacky print of Michael Caine in *Get Carter* I'd bought online.

'Oh. Yeah. I write about them.'

I picked up the three pints from the bar, and made to move away.

'Ahh. Well, then. I've worked with Mike Caine, of course. Lovely bloke. *Horse Under Water*, back in seventy-eight.'

Rod, wheezed, and turned away.

I slowly lowered the pints back onto the bar top.

'Did you say *Horse Under Water*?'

He looked over his shoulder, evidently pleased to have grabbed my attention.

'That's a Harry Palmer novel, right? Len Deighton. A sequel to the *Ipcress File*.'

'You do know it, then? Not a bad film. Tremendous fun to work on. I played a naval officer in that one, all decked out with the proper kit, scrambled egg on the hat and what have you.'

'I didn't know they'd filmed it, actually. I thought the last one they made was *The Billion Dollar Brain*. And those two TV movies in the nineties, but they don't count.'

He laughed.

'Well, they did film it. Pinewood, summer of seventy-seven.'

'Why haven't I heard about it, then?'

'Well, you learn something new every day.'

He raised his glass and downed two thirds of a pint of Stella as if it were Tizer.

That night, after dinner, I picked up *Halliwell* while I was watching TV, and flicked carelessly to where *Horse Under Water* would have been, if it existed. I grunted to myself – it wasn't there. Of course it wasn't. Just to be sure, though, I checked IMDB on my phone, and Letterboxd. Nothing there either. I smiled, and shrugged. I had worried for a moment that an important item of trivia had passed me by, but I had obviously been the victim of an imaginative old pisshead prankster.

The next time I went into The George, Rod greeted me with a wave. I waved back, but purposely ordered my drink at the other end of the bar. He slid down from his stool and, leaning on the bar the whole way, made his way along to stand at my side.

'Hello again.' He raised his glass in a salute. 'I've got something to show you.' He reached for his inside pocket – the jacket didn't have one – and then into his trouser pocket. He pulled out a dog-eared Polaroid and slapped it onto the bar, into a ring of spilled beer.

The picture showed the water tank at Pinewood with a half-formed fibre-glass submarine floating in it. In the foreground stood middle-period Michael Caine – a little doughy, thick wavy hair. He was wearing his Harry Palmer glasses and a toothy smile, alongside a younger version of my drinking companion. Caine was holding a clapperboard: HORSE UNDER WATER, 03/08/77.

I thought at first it was a Photoshop job. I picked the picture up and looked closely. If it was a fake, it was beautiful work, printed on genuine Polaroid paper and with just the right amount of fading. All the red had washed away with the years.

'Mmm.' I tried not to sound too interested. 'I couldn't find any information on this film, though.'

Rod's face fell.

'You looked it up, then? And you didn't find anything at all? Shame.'

There was something more there – not only disappointment but also, maybe, fear.

'What about these?'

He reached back into his pocket and this time retrieved a small stack of similar polaroids. He dropped the first one onto the bar. Rod and a young Timothy Dalton; in the background, a sub-James Bond set, decorated with tape-banks and steel staircases. On the clapperboard: WHO IS JERRY CORNELIUS?

'Jerry Cornelius? As in *The Final Programme*?'

'Eh?' Rod smiled absently.

'*The Final Programme*. Robert Fuest, 1973.'

'Ken Russell, 1969. I should know.'

'Are you sure? With Jenny Runacre...'

'Marianne Faithful. Here's another for you.' He looked excited, and knocked back half a pint or so, before tossing another picture onto the bar. CARRY ON ROCKING. Rod, Kenneth Williams and Freddie Starr.

'Oh, come off it! Freddie Starr was never in a Carry On film.'

'He was in *Carry On Rocking*. I should–'

'You should know, right.'

'Look.' He pointed at the photograph with a thick brown finger. '1983. Poor Ken's last Carry On. I had a speaking part in that one. You must have seen it.' He looked at me, nodding and gesturing, as if that would help me remember. Pleading.

'I've got to go. Thanks for showing me these. They're very clever.' I turned to order at the bar, and did everything I could to signal dismissal.

'There are a couple more here. This one. Do you like those old Hammer Horror pictures?'

It had to be a setup. My second book was on Hammer. I was well known as an enthusiast. Despite my suspicions, when he offered the photo, I snatched it from his hand. '*The Horror of Frankenstein*. Ralph Bates.'

'Nearly! That's Ralph alright. 1972. Read the clapper.' Rod was triumphant. He knew he had me. I admit that I was excited. The board was a little out of focus, but I held it close, and squinted. FRANKENSTEIN 1980.

I shook my head.

'I know every Hammer film made. Even the handful I haven't watched, I've seen stills.'

'Well, if that's what you think, then I will leave you be. Of course, I've got a lot more than just photos, but you wouldn't be interested in those. I don't suppose posters and props and things of that sort are in your line.' He snapped the photo from between my fingers, and scooped up the others from the bar before dropping them back into his pocket. 'Good luck with the quiz.'

'Wait, wait, Rod, just wait a moment. I need to know a bit more about your collection. I'd like a copy of that photograph, if nothing else.' The tune Wayne used to open the second half of the quiz, the theme from *Timeslip*, exploded from the struggling PA system and Rod's reply was lost in the noise. He returned to his perch, raised his glass one more time, and winked. There was something in his expression which made me feel I was failing to appreciate a very rich joke.

I was keen to talk again the following week and was disappointed not to see him when I came in from the rain an hour

Director's Cut

before the quiz began. I had spent the week scanning newspaper review archives, back issues of *Sight and Sound*, and even ringing a few people I knew through work. I hadn't come up with a single bit of evidence that any of Rod's films had ever been made.

I went up to the bar, staring at the empty stool. Eventually, I caught the landlord's eye, and beckoned him over. He was a glum looking Yorkshireman with a drooping white Teddy Boy hairdo. 'What can I get yer?'

'I was wondering if you knew... Where's Rod tonight?'

He nodded as if I'd said something wise.

'Did you know him well?'

'No, not well. We were just chatting last week.'

'It's bad news, pal. Ambulance came last weekend. He's dead.'

My legs seemed to soften in an instant, and I felt blood flood my head.

'Christ.'

'Makes you think.'

I ordered a pint and retreated to a quiet corner. I felt slightly guilty that the first thought to cross my mind had been about his collection. Who would get it? Were there relatives? What if they just threw it all away when they were clearing his flat? I jumped up, leaving my pint, and made my way back to the bar.

'Do you have a number for Rod's family? I'd like to send flowers, or a card.'

The landlord held up a finger.

'Wait one moment.'

He ducked behind the bar, and came up with a sheet of notepaper.

'Here you go. His daughter. Said to give it to anyone who was a friend of his.'

I scribbled the details into my notebook, thanked the landlord, and left the pub without drinking a drop.

I used a phone box not far from The George, and got an answer on the first ring.

'Hello?'

'Stephanie Harwood?'

'Yes.'

'I was a friend of... well, I knew your father. Rod.'

There was silence followed by throat clearing.

'I suppose you're another of his alcoholic friends from that bloody pub.'

She was far better spoken than Rod, but there was still a touch of estuary nasal in her voice.

'Well, I did meet him there, but I'm not an alcoholic.'

'People rarely recognise when they are.'

'No, really. I'm a journalist.'

'Jeffrey Barnard was a journalist.'

'I write about films,' I said, and then found myself improvising. 'I was interviewing your father for an article.'

'Oh, really?' Her voice became warmer.

'Your father was in some very unusual and interesting films, including some I didn't even know had been made.'

'Oh, well, you're in luck. He has copies of all of them, I think. Used to make me watch them when I was a child. Would you like to see them? A published article would be a lovely memorial to Dad. It's just a shame that it didn't come sooner.'

'I will do my best, Mrs Harwood, to honour your father's memory in what I write.' My performance was sentimental enough to make Tom Hanks gag.

We arranged that I would meet her, with her husband, at Rod's flat on Saturday morning, and said goodnight. My head was throbbing. Those films had not been made. I knew they hadn't. I shrugged. Saturday morning would settle it.

I arrived early and was standing drinking coffee when they pulled up in a waxed and polished BMW. Mrs Harwood was older than I had expected, with stiff orange-dyed hair and the kind of wide eyed ogling expression that contact lenses encourage. Her husband was shorter, completely bald, and wore polarised aviator glasses. When he shook my hand, his palm was cold and smooth.

The flat was above a Halal butcher, and the door was burned black and graffiti covered. There were three locks. I forced myself to stay calm, and resisted the urge to push past Mrs Harwood once the door was open. The flat smelled of antiseptic and urine and there were cat scratches all over the stair carpet. There was another door into Rod's flat itself, and this seemed to take even longer to crack, even though I suspected that a good push would have done the trick. She gestured grandly, ushering me into the sitting room.

'Please. Go ahead and have a good rummage.'

I stepped through the doorway, and whistled aloud. One wall was lined with photo albums dated from 1965 to 1993 and there were several old fashioned tea crates in the centre of the floor. I approached them first. Reaching in, I grabbed a roll of 8mm film in a Scotch box. Written on it in biro was DAN DARE, PILOT OF THE FUTURE, REEL 3, 1979. Excited, I grabbed another: BLEAK HOUSE, REEL 1. Then another: YOUNG SHERLOCK HOLMES IN NEW YORK, 1990, INCOMPLETE.

'We've got some papers to go through in the bedroom. Make yourself comfortable,' said Mrs Harwood. Mr Harwood snorted. Once they had left, I pulled out my notebook and began to write down each title as I pulled the reels out. After thirty minutes or so, Mrs Harwood shouted from the other room.

Municipal Gothic

'If you'd like to watch some of those, there's a projector in here. It's not in very good condition, but I think it works.' Mrs Harwood was clearly impressed by my enthusiasm, unlike her husband, who shouted over her: 'Load of old rubbish anyway. I suppose muggins here will have to take it all down the dump. Typical.'

'The dump?'

I walked over to the doorway with a reel in my hand, and my eyes wide with amazement. The bedroom was damp and reeked of cigarettes and stale lager. There was a well-used eight millimetre projector, and a screen on an easel, but little else. Mr and Mrs Harwood were kneeling on the floor, sifting through a stack of yellowing papers, most of which they then transferred to a bin bag. Mr Harwood looked up.

'Yeah. The dump. Where you take old things that aren't of any use anymore.'

I couldn't see his eyes behind the sunglasses, and I was glad.

'You can't do that. This collection is historically important.'

Mr Harwood's lips pulled back from slick yellow teeth.

'Don't tell me what I will and won't do, son.'

Mrs Harwood began to cry.

I carried on as if I hadn't noticed and set to work with the projector.

After a minute or two, I had *Dan Dare* threaded. My fingers were crossed as the silent, scratched image faded up. There was Nicky Henson in a sub-*Star Trek* space tracksuit, his hair hanging down around his collar and pipe in hand, piloting a poorly realised but nicely designed spaceship. Next to him, Richard Griffiths, presumably as Digby, was snivelling and doing his usual bit of business while grappling with a control lever. Cut to a treen destroyer in pursuit – Gerry Anderson's work? Cut to Rod in facepaint and a plastic vest, as a Treen commander barking orders and pressing buttons. Cut back to Henson and Griffiths; more shouting; a fizzy explosion. I was captivated. A lost British response to the *Star Wars* phenomenon. Dan Dare's ship crashed into the surface of a lush, jungle planet, and then the reel ended.

I stared at the white rectangle of light for a moment, and then exhaled.

'That was very interesting.'

'What you could see of it, through the scratches. Load of old rubbish.'

Mr Harwood looked at his watch.

'We're done. Are you going to be long?'

'I'd like to watch another, if you don't mind.'

'There's plenty of time for that later.'

Mr Harwood switched the projector off, and drew the curtains. As we left the flat, Mrs Harwood grabbed my arm.

'Sorry about my husband. He's always been jealous of Dad. To be honest, I think he's glad to have me to himself again.'

'Please don't let him do anything silly,' I pleaded.

'I'll try.' She gave me a smile, and squeezed my arm. She was flirting. I'm not used to being flirted with, but in comparison with Mr Harwood, I can see how I might have seemed appealing.

'Can I come back soon? I'll need to catalogue the films, and all the photo albums.'

'I'll see what I can do. If it was up to me…'

'Please. I'd really appreciate it.'

She pushed her hair behind her ears and nodded. Her husband whistled for her, as if for a dog.

'Are you coming, or what?'

Municipal Gothic

As the BMW pulled away, I waved limply, and lowered myself to sit on the kerb. There was every chance I was going to become a rich man, or at least famous on the cult film circuit and, despite the sheer improbability of it all, I was buzzing.

I spent the next few days carrying out some peripheral research when I should have been writing my column for *Cable and Satellite Monthly*. First, I phoned every expert on British film in my professional address book and ran some of the titles by them. 'That one rings a bell,' was a common response, but I knew that these were the Emperor's new films – no one wanted to admit they didn't know them. I took the opportunity to gloat a little: 'You haven't seen it? Oh, you should. It's a real lost classic.'

I also tried phoning agents and relatives of Michael Caine, Nicky Henson, Diana Rigg, Brigid Forbes, Nicholas Rowe, Timothy Dalton, Freddie Starr, Eric Idle, Joan Collins, Lewis Collins, Shane Bryant, Jane Asher, Marianne Faithful, John Alderton, Dennis Waterman, Paul Freeman, and a lot of other actors. Nobody was very helpful, but even those that were didn't recognise the films I was asking about.

What I couldn't understand was how Rod had managed to act *only* in films no-one had heard of. I actually had a panic attack – tight chest, near-blackout, wobbly legs – at the thought of how embarrassing this whole business could be if someone analysed the film frame-by-frame and found that it *was* a trick. Perhaps Rod was just a front for some hoaxer's elaborate con?

That Wednesday, I phoned Mrs Harwood to confirm the second viewing. Her husband answered the phone.

'Oh, it's you. I've been thinking about these films.'

I could hear him breathing across the mouthpiece of the phone, and the phlegm rattling in his throat.

'Since you seem so keen, I might be willing to let you take them off our hands.'

Director's Cut

I nearly whooped.

'That's fantastic news, Mr Harwood. I'd be happy to look after the archiving for you.'

'Calm down, son. I was thinking that, just between you and me, this might be a business transaction. Funerals aren't cheap, and that old sod sure as bloody hell didn't leave any cash behind to pay for his own do. How much?'

'I can't...'

'Well, if you can't, then I'll have to dispose of them some other way.'

He seemed to be enjoying himself. I hadn't done much bartering and gave myself away immediately.

'No! No. Right. Two hundred reels of damaged 8mm film, mostly incomplete features. That can't be worth more than...'

'I'm not a mug, sunshine. Don't waste my time.'

He ended the call. I redialled.

'Hello?'

'Mr Harwood, I was going to say that they can't be worth more than, say, two hundred pounds.'

'Two hundred quid? I might not be Jonathan Ross, but I know you think all this crap is special. I've been doing a bit of research, see? I was thinking of five grand.'

There was a long silence. I switched the phone to my other ear and cleared my throat.

'I don't have that much money. I probably never will. You're not really going to dump it all if I won't buy it, are you?'

'Maybe. Or maybe I'll sell it to someone else.' He was twisting my arm very effectively. The thought of Barry Furst, Mark Sidley or any of the others taking my story from me made me feel nauseous.

'Can I speak to your wife?' If Daddy says no, ask Mummy. The old classic. Laughter echoed down the line, sounding like a saw cutting tin. For the second time, I heard a muffled click and then silence.

I spent the afternoon trying to think of ways to get five thousand pounds together. No sources I hadn't already tapped sprang to mind. That evening, not long after I'd finished putting together an estimate of how much I could make by selling everything I owned, my phone rang.

'Hello?' I said.

It was Mrs Harwood.

'Mr Riley? Can you meet me now? My husband's out, and I thought you might want to take Dad's stuff away before he gets back.' She giggled, exhilarated. 'I feel very naughty.'

'I can't express... That's fantastic. Thank you, Mrs Harwood.'

'Please, call me Stephanie.'

She picked me up at my flat in her worn out Nissan Micra.

'We'll have to be quick. My husband will ring me when he gets home and finds I'm not there.'

'Well, he won't be too angry, will he? I mean, it's not as if we're..."

She raised her eyebrows suggestively.

'Not as if we're what?'

The evening was drawing in, and the flat was dark when we entered.

'Where's the light switch,' I whispered.

'I've brought a torch,' she replied, suddenly standing very close to me. I could smell her perfume, which was the same one my grandmother had used. She clicked the light on and shone it around the flat. The broken circle of yellow light slid across bare walls. And bare floorboards. I snatched the flashlight from her hand and jogged forward into the living room. My footsteps echoed – the room was empty.

'Where's it all gone?' I whimpered.

'Daddy's things! Where are Daddy's things?'

The torch dimmed, and went out.

'For fuck's sake!'

I pushed past her and slapped the wall around the doorway until I found the light switch. The forty watt bulb on the ceiling bloomed, illuminating an almost completely stripped room. In the middle of the floor, though, was a shoebox. I went over and knelt next to it. A note was taped to the lid.

'£200 worth of tat. Pay the wife. H.'

'Daddy's things,' said Mrs Harwood again, before wailing aloud. She launched herself toward me, rested her head on my chest and grabbed my arms with her fingers. I wasn't sure what to do, but let her sob over me without hugging back. I was in shock.

She pulled away after five minutes, leaving my t-shirt covered in warm salty water and snot.

'I'm sorry,' she said. I nodded. 'What's in the box?' she said, pointing at it.

I looked down and nodded again.

'I'll open it.' Inside was a handful of photographs – just Rod, alone, on one anonymous sound stage after another.

'Is it worth anything?' she asked hopefully, looking up at me with a contact lens stuck to her cheek.

They found Harwood's BMW later that night. Mrs Harwood called me to ask if I'd go with her to identify the body.

'I don't have anyone else, Mr Riley.'

The body on the gurney was him, alright. His bald head wasn't white anymore – it was a sticky red – but his yellow teeth still grinned from behind his shrunken lips.

I spoke to a policeman while Mrs Harwood cried.

'Looks like the daft bastard flipped a cigar out of the front window of the car and the wind whipped it in through the back window. The back seat was piled high with flammable material

– film reels, apparently. Went up like...' He gestured an explosion with his hands.

'Shit.'

'Know him well, did you?'

'No. Talked to him twice. Hated him. But it's a shame about the films. Some of them were rare.'

I laughed grimly at my own joke.

'Well, we did find a couple of reels intact.'

First the leader, then suddenly a handheld shot of the inside of a car taken from the back seat. Above the driver's seat, a shining white bald head. Euston Films aesthetic.

Cut to an exterior shot. The car passes at a leisurely pace. It's a BMW.

Cut to another car, in pursuit – a 1975 Ford Escort, being pushed hard. The driver looks familiar, but glare on the window half conceals his face.

Cut back to the BMW. The driver fiddles with the radio, and laughs. He looks startled when a horn sounds.

Cut to a POV shot from the Ford Escort. It pulls up alongside the BMW, and a hand extends. It's holding a fat cigar.

Cut to the terrified face of Mr Harwood.

Cut to Harwood's POV as a smiling mid-period Michael Caine, riding shotgun in the Escort, flicks the cigar through the open window of the BMW.

Jump-cut: the BMW exploding and careening from the road. The Escort pulls up alongside. Rod, in the driver's seat, turns to Michael Caine, and gives him a nod of approval. They pull away.

Ten Empty Rooms

One

Stock room. Basement. Dim orange streetlight glow warped through glass bricks set into the pavement above, on Back Turner Street. Bare brick walls. Ceiling of boards and beams. Stone floor, unevenly patched. A warped, mould-blackened glamour calendar displaying August 1987– 'Jeanette'. A scrap of pink carbon paper faded to blankness, smeared with oil. Broken picture frame leaning against the wall. Its glass is cracked. The photograph has been ruined by damp and spores. Five vague, smiling faces can just be made out. An unseen fingernail scrapes weakly against concrete.

Two

Sitting room. Fifth floor. White daylight through soot-crusted windows. The hum of traffic on the Finchley Road below. A single strip of floral wallpaper curls over to reveal bare plaster. Marks have been left by a thick, soft pencil – the increasing heights of two children: Judith 7.3.38, Julius 28.4.38… Spaces in black dust where pictures once hung. Stains on the carpet next to the small fireplace, marking the boundaries of a long-gone armchair. Two doors, one closed, one open onto the unlit hallway. The darkness there is unstill. The shadows shift. Something waits, shy of the light. On the floor below, a tentative note on a violin. In the empty flat there is a sigh only one degree louder than silence.

Three

Faraday Ward. First floor. Polystyrene ceiling tiles scattered and shattered on the linoleum. Bindweed grows through the window frames and across the yellow-painted walls. No beds, no visitors' chairs, no bedside tables. The built-in clock above the swing doors stopped many years ago. Water has come in through the roof and knocks insistently on the floor. Over the course of years it has formed a ring – yellow-green on the outside, bruise black at the centre. Hours pass until daylight begins to fade. There is a squeal. The doors swing open, swing back, screech, slowed by their own decaying springs. They judder back into their resting position.

Four
The kitchen of a semi-detached house overlooking a garden smothered by brambles, imprisoning the rotten remains of a summer house and a set of rusting swings. The doors of the fitted cabinets and drawers, lined with scraps of wallpaper, hang open. Tiles that were once white, now grey, are stained with cat food in the corner by the back door. Dark lines recall the absent fridge, table, dresser and washing machine. The only sound is of mice chewing and running behind the skirting boards. A dead lightbulb hangs from the ceiling. It moves slowly from side to side as if caught in a breeze, though the air is stale and still.

Five
Studio flat. Third floor. Perfectly clean, newly painted, flat white walls and pristine mushroom-grey carpet. One large space with a minimal kitchen at the deep end. Only the bathroom has its own door. Hard sunlight through a skylight sketches a bright square on the floor. Over the course of the afternoon it slides along and up the wall. Then moonlight repeats the performance, this time in blue. From the corner where the shadow is most dense comes a sound like cotton brushing bare skin. Then something less than a whisper, close but far away, then something less than laughter, then fragile silence.

Six

Warehouse number two. Stripped bare, ready for demolition. Dirty yellow daylight through the corrugated PVC roof, which replaced a Victorian original after the Blitz. Pigeons flutter against the ceiling. Rats run through the tide of scraps and cigarette ends around the edges of the space. As the building rots, every small sound triggers an answering echo: plaster falls from the walls, pipes drip, fittings shrink and swell. Sometimes, there are footsteps, too, or something like them, or maybe nothing like them, although if you knew Gerry Mills when he was foreman, you might think you recognised the sound.

Seven

Public toilet. Far side of the park. Bricked up. Frosted windows with frames painted council green. Fired tiles, their surfaces crazed and chipped, cover the walls and floor. Scraps of a poster offer a ten pound reward for reports of vandalism. Another, high on the wall, says: 'Did you know V.D. can be cured?' Outside, there are the sounds of traffic, dance music, children playing, birdsong and barking dogs. Inside, only the creak of ceiling beams as they expand in midday summer heat. There are three cubicles, two without doors. The third door is still there and almost closed. Through the gap, perhaps the wet glint of an eye.

Eight

Office. Sixth floor. Painted on the frosted glass of the door is the name of a company whose owner comes here once a week to collect post and check the answerphone. No desk, no filing cabinets, no stock – just a telephone balanced on the windowsill over an ancient radiator and a single plastic school chair. Every time the wind gusts across the moor, the plastic vent set into the window flaps its louvres and the frame whines or whistles. Once or twice a year, the telephone gets thrown to the floor or, as now, the chair suddenly judders and scrapes a metre across the floorboards, with painful effort.

Nine

Classroom. Second floor. Windows covered with steel to keep out squatters. Thin beams of white light through pencil-hole perforations casting constellations on the far wall. That's the wall with scraps of drawings and projects – blue ink faded to brown, felt-tip pen colours washed away to near nothing. No chairs, no tables and only screw holes where bookcases were once fixed in place. The blackboard is blank, not black, scuffed to grey. From certain angles, chalk marks can be seen in the dust. Digit-thick, clumsy, but unmistakable: words, a name, some feeble attempt to reach across.

Ten

Executive suite. First floor. Notices on yellowing plastic ask guests to reuse their towels and notify them of the fire drill. No bed. No chair. Just a plush headboard in purple Velveteen screwed to the wall and a single lace curtain dangling from a rod. The curtain ripples in the razor-sharp breeze that seeps through a crack in the window. Through the glass, a blank wall on the other side of the alley, wet with black-green slime. The carpet has more stains than pure colour and grooves where furniture sat for thirty years. In the low, cold light, something flickers into being and, for the length of a blink, the room isn't empty at all.

Who Took Mary Cook?

Eve was driving to work when she saw the graffiti for the first time, its vicious white letters stretched across the concrete of the pedestrian bridge on The Highway:

WHO TOOK MARY COOK?

It flustered her. It felt like an accusation. She thought about pulling over and walking back, or performing a U-turn at the next gap in the central verge. Anxious to clock in on time, though, she did neither. By the time she reached the factory gates she was convinced she'd imagined it.

Who on the estate even remembered Mary Cook? Nobody. Hers wasn't one of those cases that got dredged up or dramatised. There was no famous photograph of Mary that appeared on newspaper front pages in murky halftones. Her family didn't make tearful appeals on birthdays or anniversaries.

Still distracted, Eve swung into the car park and took a space near the smoking shelter. She turned the key to stop the engine but didn't get out of the car.

Mary Cook.

Eve hadn't thought about the little girl with the protruding teeth in years.

That fearfully hot summer day in 1976, when she was eighteen.

The moment Eve opened the front door and stepped onto the oil-spotted path, she could tell something was wrong – that the estate was running a fever. The silence was fat, as if the engine of a flying bomb had just cut out in the blue sky above and everyone was braced for impact.

Closing the gate behind her, slipping the frayed rope over the post which served in lieu of the missing metal catch, Eve walked up Longwood Road fully alert, excited, amid the smell of the drains and with Maria's ice cream van distantly stumbling around the notes of its music-box tune.

Up ahead, not quite out of sight, she perceived the pulsing of a blue light and quickened her step.

The lawns she passed were brown and brittle, littered with plastic paddling pools and faded deck-chairs. Even the weeds growing between the paving stones were wilting. A cluster of silver-winged ants crawled drunkenly around the concrete lamp-post on the corner of Orchard Road. A woman in a yellow apron was pouring the contents of a kettle over a black mass on her front doorstep, the steam rising up to redden her face. The woman's glasses fogged and she paused to wipe condensation from her forehead.

There were several police cars, baby blue and white, but also unmarked, around the junction of Longwood and Vauxhall roads. There were policemen and women standing on doorsteps and marching along the pavements supervised by detectives with their sleeves rolled up, sweat staining their shirts. There was no ambulance.

Slowing, Eve made eye contact with a police constable who was about to open the gate of number twenty-six. He looked over her summer clothes and pale skin and stopped, giving a half smile. He was grey, thin and old, shrinking away inside the heavy wool of his uniform tunic which did not apparently cause him any discomfort despite the heat. His head was too small for the helmet that half-obscured his eyes.

'Good afternoon, miss.'

'What's going on?'

'Do you live nearby?'

She nodded.

'I'd like to ask you a few questions, if I may.'

'Of course.'

'Do you know a young lass called Mary Cook?'

'Not to talk to but, uh, yes. What's happened?'

She was one of the children, between seven and twelve years old, who played on the green on the corner of Longwood Road and Vauxhall Road. They were a mass, not a group of individuals. Scuffed shoes, shirt tails and snot, constantly spitting and sniffing their fingers. Mary did stand out, though. She was neater and prettier. Eve pictured her hanging back from the play that inevitably turned into fighting, running back and forth and bouncing on her heels, excited to be near the game but not really in it. Her mother, Annette, had been a few years ahead of Eve at school and worked in the canteen at the factory. They spoke almost every day over the warming pans – 'Fish is good today, love.' Annette worried about Mary because she was thin and dreamy, and sucked her thumb which was no good for her teeth. When she smiled, they stuck out like the protective shards of pottery on a garden wall.

'And when would you say you last saw her, miss?'

'I don't know. This week, probably. Maybe last. Playing tag or kiss chase or something. Is she missing, then?'

The policeman nodded gravely.

'Not been seen since yesterday afternoon. Have you noticed anyone suspicious around? Anyone you don't recognise?'

'There's never anyone new. Who'd come to Longwood if they didn't live here?'

'If you think of anything, talk to me or one of my colleagues, or phone the station.'

Eve walked on, slowly now, half-dazed. Nothing had changed, not really, but the sunlight seemed tarnished, the air gritty in her mouth.

All the way along the road people were standing in their front gardens, partly to enjoy the hum and scent of summer, but also because the estate, as a body, was restless. Who could sit inside watching TV when a question had been asked, but no answer given?

Eve muttered subdued greetings to Mr Glover in his boiler suit and Mrs Glover in her pinny; to the widowed Mr Pear who wore his trilby and polyester sports jacket despite the heat; and to Pam Barnicoat who had her two boys, five and seven, pinned to her long denim-clad legs. The children looked solemn, picking up on the anxiety of the adults.

'Terrible business, about the girl,' said Pam in reply to Eve's greeting.

Eve stopped and leaned lightly on the rotting wooden gate.

'I expect she's just run away,' she said, unconvincingly. 'I used to do that all the time when I was a kid.'

Pam grimaced and pulled at a hair protruding from the mole on her chin.

'She was seen,' she said.

Eve felt a jolt and, guiltily, a desperate desire to know more.

'They didn't tell me that.'

'Well, they're not telling anyone but, between you and me, it was Rita that saw her.'

Pam nodded in the direction of number forty.

'She was with a man, on that dead-end road up by the fields.'

'What man?'

Pam shrugged and pulled her mouth into a sour clench.

'Just a man, Rita says.' Pam looked about slyly, not wanting to be heard. 'Probably one of those Polish blokes they've got working at BPL these days. Away from their wives... And they're all Catholics. You know what they're like.'

She looked down at her own boys and tightened her grip on them.

A bar or two of electric organ music came from the upper floor of number forty-four – a 'A Taste of Honey', all bass pedal and reedy high notes, wobbling with tremolo, backed by a Bossa Nova beat.

'I'll never know how he got that bloody thing up those stairs,' said Pam with a tut. 'Day and night he's on it. It's like living next door to a circus.'

Eve smiled uncomfortably and glanced up at the open steel-framed window. She thought of the hands on the keyboard with their pink flesh and yellow nails and felt sick.

After five minutes watching rain trace lines on the windscreen, Eve looked in the rear-view mirror, pushed a curl of grey hair behind her ear, and got out of the car.

Inside the factory, she changed into her overalls, said a distracted 'Hello' to Donna, to Kerry and to the baby-faced trainee whose name she couldn't recall. She drank a small, bitter coffee from the vending machine and, at exactly 8:59, swiped her card through the reader.

They put her on the packing line which meant she was effectively alone, wrapped in the sound of the conveyor. As her fingers folded and sealed box after box of BPL Evershine Silver-cream, she couldn't stop thinking about Mary Cook. She struggled sometimes to picture her own late brother but Mary came to her with the clarity of a freshly-developed Polaroid. In the snapshot she had, Mary was turning to laugh against a black background full of sparkling lights – perhaps it was something she had seen at a Christmas party at the long-closed factory social club, she thought.

He would have been there, at the party, playing the organ or playing records. Flared trousers, wiry hair in his ears, teeth the colour of butter.

She shook her head, squeezed her eyes closed.

The conveyor belt stopped and a bell rang.

'You alright, Evie?'

'What's the matter, love?'

'Nothing, nothing, just a headache.'

As the day drew to a close, Eve felt a sense of dread. She didn't want to see the graffiti again. Still, as her little hatchback passed under the bridge she glanced in the rear-view mirror.

'Thank god,' she said.

The words had gone, the concrete scrubbed back to raw grey by council workmen, she assumed.

She needed a tin of soup for tea, bread and milk so she stopped at the Costcutter on the way home. The kids who loitered there ignored her as she dashed into the shop, around it, and out.

They didn't notice that she stopped and jolted, her brown eyes fixed on the blank wall beyond the parking bays and the road.

Above the painted goalposts, above the painted wicket, surrounded by tags and scrawls, there it was again:

WHO TOOK MARY COOK?

It was smaller than the paintwork on the bridge but there was no less fury in its strokes. Had it been there when she pulled up? Dazed, she crossed the road and reached up to run her fingers over the letters. The paint was dry – flaking and faded, in fact, as if it had been there a long time.

'Oi, missus – who's Mary Cook?' shouted one of the teenagers through a cloud of grape-flavoured vape.

'I don't know,' she said. 'Why are you asking me?'

Eve avoided the shops for a few days but when she next drove by, on her way to the factory just before dawn had fully broken, she saw that the question was gone. She parked, jerking the handbrake up, and stumbled across to the wall. In the green light of the shop window, she ran her hand over the brick. There was no sign anything had ever been painted there.

'You alright, love?'

It was an old man in yellow-tinted glasses and tracksuit bottoms, carrying a copy of the *Daily Mail*.

'No, yes, I'm fine, thanks – I was just...'

She hadn't been sleeping and her eyes were raw.

'They paint all sorts there, don't they? I live over there and I hear 'em at it in the middle of the night, those cans they use.'

Eve stepped closer.

'Who took Mary Cook?' she said.

'What's that, love? I'm half deaf.'

'Who took Mary Cook? It was written on the wall.'

He shook his head.

'I'd have noticed that.' He made a move towards his house but continued to speak over his shoulder. 'Mary Cook? Wasn't she that girl that went missing twenty years back?'

'Forty years ago,' said Eve.

'Was it, be damned? Time flies, doesn't it?'

He waved his newspaper and waddled away.

For six months, through autumn and into winter, Mary Cook's disappearance set the mood on the estate. There were more police patrols than usual, panda cars cruising and officers in plain clothes knocking on doors at unexpected times.

Search parties swished through the tall grass of the fields behind the estate, overturning adders' nests and sacks of dumped rubbish. They dug through drainage ditches, opened water tanks and poked through barns, sheds and lean-tos. The barking of sniffer dogs sounded through the fog.

Television crews and newspaper reporters came, looking for local colour, but soon went when they didn't find it. The grey estate with its estate problems had no juice.

Posters on telegraph poles and community centre notice boards – 'Have you seen this girl?' – faded and feathered away as the months passed.

People couldn't help but gossip and, one by one, every man on the estate drifted into the frame, then out again. Pete Barnicoat was taken in for questioning and released after three days; Pam Barnicoat left with the children a week later. Mr Glover, old Mr Pear, the Blythe Brothers, Gordon Cornock with his limp and lazy eye, Mavis Newick's Polish lodger – all, for a moment, definitely did it, until they definitely didn't. 'I always said there was something funny about him – you can see it in his eyes.'

Eve didn't get involved because she assumed at some point they'd get to the man at number forty-four and find out for themselves what he was like. Or maybe she was wrong, maybe he wasn't like that – perhaps she'd done something to encourage him. People seemed to like him, despite the boozy breath and the grubby cuffs on his mustard-coloured jacket. She waited and watched but it never happened. He just kept playing 'Sugar, Sugar' and 'The Air That I Breathe', polishing his Hillman Hunter, winking at passers-by through clouds of cigarette smoke.

Christmas came and an unspoken collective decision was made: we can't mourn or fret forever; let's leave it here. Among the fairy lights and crates of light ale, Mary Cook disappeared for a second time.

In the spring of 1977, the Cook family moved away.

And Eve, to her shame, was glad.

Driving to and from work, in and out of town and the supermarket, Eve found herself scanning walls, bridges and underpasses. Was she hoping to see it, or hoping not? She kept an eye on the local news, too, in case someone came forward to explain. Maybe others had seen the painted messages and investigated. Mary Cook had brothers and a sister. Perhaps they or someone else in the family had decided to 'raise awareness' with a publicity campaign on the fortieth anniversary of Mary's disappearance.

After a fortnight with no repeat incident, the tension in her shoulders eased. She pushed Mary and the man at number forty-four back down into the far part of her memory and began to make space for other thoughts. There was a trip to London to plan for one thing – half-term with her grandson, trips to museums and pretending to drive the Docklands Light Railway.

She had spent Saturday morning cleaning and cooking, listening to Sounds of the Sixties on Radio 2, when the words appeared again. First, Tony Blackburn announced 'I Can't Help Myself', which should have been warning enough – it was one of the songs the man at forty-four played, winking when he sang 'sugar pie, honeybunch'. She rushed to switch off the radio, squeezing the unresponsive rubber buttons on the remote and, as silence fell, dropped into her well-worn armchair with eyes closed. She sighed and then slowly lifted her eyelids. Her hands gripped the fabric of the seat and she let out a small, cracked yelp.

There it was, across the blank stretch of Dulux Hint of Daffodil, this time in ripe, running red:

WHO TOOK MARY COOK?

Nobody was there and even if they had been, there wouldn't have been time for them to paint the words.

'I don't know,' she said aloud. 'I don't know who took her.'

Lying didn't help. The words didn't burn away. They stared her down.

She rushed to get soap, water and a J-cloth from the cupboard under the kitchen sink.

When she returned, the wall was blank.

Summer 1977 came.

Old Mr Pear, who never quite recovered from the shock of being questioned by the police, died in his sleep and a young couple with a baby moved into the vacant council flat.

Winter, summer, winter, summer.

The Glovers had another kid – an accident, of course.

And the organist from number forty-four married a widow he met through a classified ad in The Stage *and moved away.*

Eve could breathe again.

In 1980, she married a warehouseman called David and moved into one of the red-brick new-builds on the private estate they'd built on open country where the police once searched for Mary Cook.

Winter, summer, winter, summer...

Eve had a child, two children, three children, and stray grey hairs began to appear. She had it hacked back to rough spikes which was safer for the production line anyway, and cheaper to look after. Her hands got rough and her nails grew short.

More winters, more summers.

David's occasional whisky chaser on Friday night became whisky every night, and then whisky at breakfast, until Eve sent him away.

Winters, summers.

Eve's father died a month after retiring; mother managed two more years; David was found dead on the floor of his caravan a month after he turned thirty-eight.

Long shadows, midday sun.

The kids left one after the other – army and Afghanistan, university and London, drugs and Australia. Sometimes they called.

Occasionally they came home for Christmas, or invited her to stay, but not often enough.

And Eve, hard as concrete, just kept getting up and going to work.

What else was there to do?

Next, Eve began to hear the words. First, it was just the echo of their playground rhyme, in her moonlit bedroom. She held her breath and listened to her own pulse, certain she'd just missed a shout that had snapped her from sleep.

Driving to work, bunged up and weary, she heard them as a four-note commercial radio jingle.

Shaken by spring gales, trees whispered it to her.

The machinery at work gave the words rhythm: WHO, TOOK, MARY, COOK?

At home, with all the lights on and television turned up high, she still heard the house muttering in her ear, demanding an answer to a simple question – insisting that she break her silence.

Soon, it was her own voice she could hear, murmuring the phrase over and over as if trying to memorise it.

Finally, Mary arrived to ask the question herself: 'Who took me, Eve? Where did he take me?'

There she stood, in flared jeans, Clarks shoes and grass-stained striped top. Her teeth, gapped and angled, glistened.

'You know who,' said Eve.

Where were they? In the front room of Eve's house, or maybe her parents' house, or perhaps his house – number forty-four. A distant organ, drifting out of tune, played 'When I Kissed the Teacher'. A nowhere place, the slippery terrain at the edge of a dream.

Mary asked again, pleading, and Eve stretched her mouth open, fighting the gravity of her nightmare.

Snapping awake, knocking over a stick glass with an inch of gin in the bottom, she shouted his name – said it aloud for the first time in four decades.

Don Willmott, the man from number forty-four, the Hammond organ maestro, was a salesman.

He knew what people needed, what they were missing, and how to make them want what he was selling. Eve wanted to be spoken to like a grown-up. She wanted to be admired. Don Willmott, with his glasses of sherry and silk shirts, seemed sophisticated and had a way of looking at her as if she was peculiarly fascinating.

He let her listen to his records – the latest singles, delivered in batches every Monday, ready to be played at the social club and The Britannia Inn every weekend. After a while, though, he became uneasy about having her at the house.

'You'll make people jealous, darling,' he said. So they started meeting at the allotment, in the shed, with its two deckchairs and a bottle of gin. A charm bracelet as a present, a song in her ear as she sat on his lap: 'Sugar, sugar…' Then he claimed what he thought he'd earned.

She tried to tell her mother who refused to hear it. Like everyone else, especially women, she liked Mr Willmott with his constant smile, clear blue eyes and readiness with a compliment.

'You shouldn't be teasing men,' she said. 'I won't tell your father what you've been up to.'

Eve drove through the silent streets knowing what had to be done.

The allotment gates were locked but Eve was ready for that. She brought the rusty old hammer down with both hands and the padlock popped. In the light from her phone, she crashed through canes and cabbages, sinking into newly-turned earth, knowing exactly where she needed to be.

Don Willmott's shed was still there. Don Willmott still used it.

Another padlock, another hammer blow, and Eve was inside. Mice scattered. She tossed watering cans, tarpaulin and twine through the open door.

The floorboards, brittle and bowed, came up easily with the claw-end of the hammer.

In the space beneath there were stacks of magazines, videotapes and sealed cardboard boxes. And between them, wrapped in shreds of striped cotton and denim, there were bones.

An Oral History of the Greater London Exorcism Authority

Sir Francis Cockerell, GLEA chairman 1977-1982

It all started with Enfield, didn't it? After Janet we were suddenly up to our eyeballs in poltergeists. Couldn't move for tenants claiming their favourite teacup had been broken and, of course, could they be moved nearer to their dear old mother at Bellingham, please? And you can trace Enfield back to *The Exorcist*, I suppose. Gave people ideas. Anyone can spew up some soup, put on a pantomime voice, smash a vase. Anyone. We had to put a stop to it. As I say, it became an epidemic. The politicians wanted us to call in the church. Most of them still professed, as it were, to 'believe'. But we said, ah, no, we won't do that. What we will do is gather the boffins.

Dr Rebecca Roberts, chief psychologist with the GLEA 1977-1986

As I argued in my first book *The Haunted Generation*, which was based on the research I did with Dr Selmhorst in Utrecht during 1975, I believe our present poltergeist problem is what you might call a symptom of the 'Long' Second World War. Across the western world, if I might employ that shorthand, we have young people born without fathers, or mothers, or with parents traumatised in various ways, to various degrees, by the experience. In young men, this manifested primarily as violence. Look towards America and its rash of serial murders or, indeed, our own football hooligans. In young women, the response was different. More romantic, one might almost say.

An expression of powerlessness within the confines of a dominant patriarchy. So-called poltergeist activity.

Sir Francis Cockerell
Dr Roberts suggested that we humour them. She'll describe in more elaborate terms than that, I daresay, but that was the gist. It was a theatrical exercise.

Dr Rebecca Roberts
The approach was built on established therapeutic techniques, founded on empathy. Our thinking was that if we responded with apparent sincerity and played into the romantic narrative at which they were the centre – that they were the special focus of a malignant spirit – claimants would feel heard and be mollified. The 'haunting' would end. The frauds, on the other hand, would have the opportunity to make a dignified climbdown from the lies they had told, to the same ends.

Ken Trapnell, special effects modelmaker
I'd done a supposed ghost-neutralising machine for a film called *The Haunting of Death House* for Amicus in '73, with Roy Ward Baker, and I suppose that's how they heard of me. I based the GLEA-EP93 on that. The important thing was that it had to look and feel weighty. Solid. So, for one thing, we slung a great lump of concrete inside the box. Then it had to look as if it was responding to external stimulus, to feel alive, as it were, so we rigged the dials to respond to sound and tremors. The operator could also set off an alarm using a radio remote. Very effective in action.

Dr Rebecca Roberts
The vans, the uniforms, the logo, the paperwork – all of this had to signal that we were taking this every bit as seriously as the householders. The Design Research Unit offered some advice

on logos, typography, and so on. 'Official blandness' was the phrase they used, if I recall correctly. The biggest challenge was convincing the field operatives to play it straight. A touch of the Milgram experiment.

Ernest 'Cabbage' Lacomber, field engineer 1977-1978

You felt stupid, do you know what I mean? I didn't believe in ghosts then and I knew the machine was a con. And you're telling me I've got to stand there with my clipboard and talk to some dozy old... I've got to stand there with a straight face? But the Prof explained that was what made it work. The placebo effect. What she said, and this has always stuck with me, is that if you put it across, you know... If you project enough authority, people will believe whatever you say.

Irene Shelper, GLEA helpline manager 1977-1981

I had previously been at Hackney Council on the housing support line and of course it was a similar class of person, if you know what I mean, with actually rather similar types of queries. I had, in fact, in that role, spoken to more than one tenant who claimed to have seen or heard something untoward in a council flat. The GLEA was just another job to me, really – just more of the same. One comes in each day, one briefs the girls, one steps in to provide support with more complicated clients. There were just two girls at first, both transferred from the GLC secretarial pool, as I recall, and I must say, we were remarkably busy from day one.

Cathy Vitali and Sandra Haward, telephone operators

CV: Mrs Shelper used to say that there were more flies caught with honey than vinegar and they were mostly very nice people. Just scared. Or confused.

SH: Cracked, you mean, Cath.

CV: A lot of people with broken homes or, you know, fathers who drank. I'd just try to listen, be sympathetic.

SH: We had a script, didn't we? To try to talk them out of it, I suppose you'd say. Sometimes, just telling us about it seemed to help. Like…

CV: Getting it off their chests.

SH: Yes. But if they were absolutely adamant – they could get quite shirty, actually, if they were in the middle of an incident – we'd take their details on a form B-107, book an appointment and then pass the information on to the boys.

'Cabbage' Lacomber

I'd been on drains and gutters before this and it was pretty similar. Clock in, check the worksheet, sign out a van and off you go. 'Where's the problem then, love? Upstairs is it? Yes please, two sugars.' – all that. Lug the machine up, plug it in – 'Is that coming off my electric?' Bloody hell! You'd take a few measurements – temperature, humidity – write them on the B-103, then run the machine for a bit. Afterwards, you'd redo the measurements and say, 'Oh, yes, there you go – definite improvement there. Shouldn't think you'll have any trouble now.' And it bloody worked. We'd get these letters thanking us so much for what we'd done, how we'd saved their lives. Look, it was steady work with happy customers – what's not to like?

Sir Francis Cockerell
Marvellous results. Absolutely wonderful. Significant return on investment. The newspapers made mischief, of course.

Tony Carman, staff writer at the Evening Standard, 1968-1987
Local government funding ghost hunters? Loved it. Fantastic stuff. Ticked all the boxes for me – waste of public money, world gone mad, you couldn't make it up! It started out as a couple of 'it's a wacky old world' box-outs on page fifteen but I think we realised quite early on it was a story with legs.

Chris Sitwell, Metropolitan Police 1975-1983
I was just off probation and on the beat in Camberwell throughout 1978. On the morning of the second of September that year, which was a Saturday, at around eight o'clock, I was making my way past Cornwall House on Emmanuel Road when I saw a young woman in a nightdress waving from the second storey, calling out for help. I proceeded at haste to the flat in question, finding it in considerable disarray. The young woman, one Mrs Donna Kelly, informed me that the furniture had tipped by itself, that plates and cups had flown from the shelves and that her son had been thrown from his bed. The child was unharmed, as far as I could see. I detected no trace of alcohol on her breath and her pupils were not dilated. I took notes and said that, regrettably, as no crime had been committed, there was nothing I could do. Then I remembered I'd seen this story in the paper and assisted her in ascertaining the number for the GLEA hotline.

Irene Shelper

Yes, I remember Mrs Kelly. I have nothing to say on the matter. Other than that I'm sure all of us regret what happened to the boy. Speaking for myself, I should say, rather, I am personally very sorry about that.

Cathy Vitali

I took the first call from Donna. It wasn't anything special. I do remember asking her about the family situation, which was one of the things on the questionnaire, and she told me her husband had left shortly before the first incident. She wanted to move flats but I said, 'Why don't we send someone round and see what can be done first? It's a lot of trouble moving house, you know.' This was all in the script.

Adrian Keefe, GLEA field engineer 1978-1979

I started in August '78. Army before that, Ireland and Germany. Donna Kelly was one of my first call-outs after finishing training. We went into two-man teams, partly because the machine was so heavy, partly because the union insisted on it. Three flights of stairs we had to get it up with no lift – and it was hot, too, sort of Indian summer kind of thing. Me and Nev [Hutchinson] standing there covered in sweat, gasping for air. Donna opens the door and I swear I could feel the cold coming out, like a walk-in freezer.

Neville Hutchinson, GLEA field engineer 1978-1983

I don't believe in nothing like that. I believe in God and Jesus and the Bible but not ghosts. I felt the cold, though, sure. Didn't faze me. We set up the machine in the boy's bedroom, because that's where she said it felt worst.

Adrian Keefe

That room was colder again. I grew up in a prefab in Catford and that got really cold in the winter, ice on the windows. And it was like that. Like winter. And Donna you could tell was terrified. Nervous breakdown territory.

Neville Hutchinson

Nobody was paying me to be a therapist. Nobody was paying me enough to ask questions. We set up the machine, took the measurements and turned it on. We let it run.

Adrian Keefe

While the machine was running, that's when I heard it, the voice. An old woman, I thought. Nev heard it too.

Neville Hutchinson

I didn't hear nothing, for the record.

Dr Rebecca Roberts

I've often wondered about the voice Adrian Keefe claims to have heard. Later on, we did equip our engineers with tape recorders and even video equipment but not at that early stage. In my view, nothing Adrian reported was inconsistent with Donna producing those sounds herself.

Adrian Keefe

We switched off the machine, maybe a bit sooner than usual, twenty minutes rather than the usual thirty, and I went through the script. Donna just looked at me as if I was bloody mad. I'm saying, there you go, should be sorted now, and we can both feel that the room, if anything, has got colder. Then the machine switches itself back on, starts rocking. Nev yanked the cable out of the wall and said, 'We'd better get going.' So we gave her a chit and went.

Neville Hutchinson

It was just normal. A normal job. I went back to the canteen, ate a fry-up, never thought twice about it again.

Dr Rebecca Roberts

Donna was, and is, a complex personality. There was a tendency, I think, to regard her as a rather placid, inarticulate young woman. It's true that she was poorly-educated – she left school at fifteen, pregnant with Gerard. But in the time I spent with her, I saw evidence of a febrile imagination and a certain sharpness that, in my view, she had been conditioned to conceal. Her father was an alcoholic bully who left the family and became a vagrant when she was twelve. Her mother also drank and was frequently unpredictable and violent. Donna entered into a relationship with Yannis Nikolaides when she was fourteen and he was already twenty. He was abusive towards her and a habitual user of drugs. The man she married, and whose name she took, was also violent and left her when the child was five. There was a great deal of unhappiness bottled up in her – and a lot of unexpressed anger.

Cathy Vitali

She called back the next day, absolutely hysterical, poor thing. I said, look, give it another day or two for things to settle down, which was what we'd been trained to say. Sandra spoke to her the next morning – she'd been trying to get through since dawn, hadn't slept.

Sandra Haward

She was a bit simple. Like talking to a child, really, except her language was atrocious. Eff this, eff that. She said the lights were going on and off, she'd seen a… What did she call it? A 'shadow man'. Her purse disappeared and came back. Writing in lipstick on the mirror in the bathroom.

Cathy Vitali

She must have called twenty times that day. Mrs Shelper was all for logging her as a 'persistent nuisance' and having the GPO put a block on her number at the exchange. It was when she said the boy had started to show bruises that we said, no, enough is enough, we'd better send round a social worker. They said that would take several days and so Mrs Shelper said, fine, we'll send round a senior engineer in the meantime, to make her, Donna, feel a bit better.

'Cabbage' Lacomber

I'd never believed in any of it before. I'm about as spiritual as a weekend at Butlin's, know what I mean? But Cornwall House was different. I turn up with my clipboard, right, and my best tie – this would have been about four thirty in the afternoon, last job of the day – and straight away I can see which flat it is I'm supposed to go to. The lights are flickering, for starters, and the door's open onto the balcony. I go up and as I get near, I feel this arctic bloody wind come out. The sound is like… You know when there's a train coming round the bend? You can't quite hear the train but the rails are sort of humming. Like that. I knock, 'Hello missus,' all that, and she says, 'Come in', so I start to go in, right? But I can't. I can't bring myself to do it. So I shout out again, 'Why don't you come with me, love?' I'm shaking, quivering, like a greyhound with stage fright, right? I wait for her to come out with the boy and a bag and I take her home with me. The next day, I put in my report, and asked for a transfer back to drains.

Sir Francis Cockerell

Astonishing. I laughed, at first, then thought, oh no – what on earth are we supposed to do now? We simply had no mechanism for dealing with such an eventuality. Every system, every process, was devised on the base understanding that the tenants were either deluded or dishonest. When one of our own operatives declares that, in his opinion, there is real cause for concern, are we to trust him?

Dr Rebecca Roberts

Mr Lacomber's account of what he saw did nothing to change my mind. It was September. The temperature typically drops in the early evening. And, of course, there was the newspaper interview which perhaps suggests a motive for dishonesty.

Tony Carman

The GLEA had become my beat – 'Bit short on page four today, get Tony to do one of his stories about the council ghost hunters!' So when I bumped into a bloke I knew from the *Express* one liquid lunchtime at the Cheshire Cheese, he told me he'd been speaking to Ernie Lacomber about this business at a flat in Camberwell. Didn't want to cover it himself, not his turf, but thought I might be interested. I got Ernie's address, out in Acton or Neasden or somewhere like that, and jumped in a cab.

'Cabbage' Lacomber

It wasn't for money, believe me. It was for Donna and because I thought people ought to know.

Tony Carman

I sat in Cabbage's sitting room, plastic cover on the sofa, print of the Chinese Girl over the fireplace, and listened to him talk for thirty, forty minutes. It wasn't what he said so much as how he said it. Just absolute sincerity. And I thought, first, this is bollocks, isn't it? Because ghosts don't exist. Then, secondly, shit, this isn't the story I've been telling. My story was that the GLEA was a stupid waste of money because, as I say, there's no such thing as ghosts. Now, suddenly, it's that the GLEA is a stupid waste of money because ghosts do exist but they can't do anything about it. It's a fraud.

'Cabbage' Lacomber

Then Mrs L calls Donna down. She's been sleeping for two days straight, more or less, and she looks a lot better. We introduce her to Mr Carman and she tells him the whole thing – how it started, what she'd seen, the voices, Gerard's bruises. Now, Carman's a wily sod, and you can see his brain turning over, working out the angles, know what I mean? I told him not to use my name.

'Family left to rot in haunted council flat', *Evening Standard*, Wednesday 4 October 1978

Donna Kelly believes her flat in Camberwell is haunted. There's no doubting that. She also believed that the GLC's £10 million ghost-hunting service might be able to help. Instead, she was patronised, ignored and left to fend for herself as someone, or something, battered her 8-year-old son black and blue.

On a cold Tuesday evening I visited the flat myself, alone, with Ms. Kelly's permission. I found squalor aplenty, as well as evidence of unsafe electrics and life-threatening black mould. I heard no voices, saw no shadowy figures and felt no shivers down my spine. It's no wonder the GLEA hasn't been able to help.

For one thing, their machine does nothing, and at great expense I might add, as one of their own engineers confirmed when I spoke to him earlier this week. 'We sent in a boy to do a man's job,' he said. 'What I saw in that flat isn't anything the council can fix. It's the Vatican they need.'

Perhaps he's right. More immediately, council tenants like Donna Kelly deserve proper housing and to be treated with respect, not conned by men in boiler suits. London's ratepayers deserve more, too.

Sir Francis Cockerell

At this point, I simply wanted the story to go away, so we gave Mrs Kelly what she wanted – a new house elsewhere in London. Precisely the kind of thing the scheme was intended to prevent, of course. Most frustrating. Why these people can't simply put themselves on the transfer list and wait I will never know.

Tony Carman

Nectar! Absolute nectar! They thought it would shut the story down but what they'd done was admit there was something in it. One way or the other. I was triumphant – 'Standard wins new home for young mum' and so on.

Irene Shelper

We were somewhat busy on the phone lines for a few weeks afterwards.

Cathy Vitali

It was madness, wasn't it, Sandra? Every poor bugger who didn't like their flat or house thought, here we go–

Sandra Haward

All change!

Irene Shelper

I found it most interesting that the family which moved into Mrs Kelly's flat in Camberwell did not call us.

Dr Rebecca Roberts

I called on them after they'd been in the flat for a month or so. It had been renovated and repainted and was rather pleasant. Good light. I presented myself as a housing worker from Lambeth Council as I was keen to avoid upsetting them or suggesting... Well, I suppose I didn't want to give them ideas. As it happened, they were well aware of the flat's reputation.

Diane Murray, resident of Cornwall House 1980-91

Neil and I – that's my late husband – we thought it was hilarious. Neither of us was religious or spiritual. We were young, had a sense of humour about most things, a bit mischievous, I suppose. If it was a choice between a flat with a ghost, and one without... Give us the ghost, please, everytime! But it wasn't a choice. We needed a flat near my mum so she could look after the baby when I went back to work and this was the only one going. Oh, yeah, we thought it was very funny. And it was a lovely flat. We were very happy. Apart from it being where Neil died, I think very fondly of it, as does my daughter. Full of laughter it was, always.

Cathy Vitali

How long would you say it was, Sand, before we heard from Donna again? Six months?

Sandra Haward

That'd be about right. Things had just settled down again, back to the old routine, when I pick up the phone, do my spiel, and I look over at you, don't I? And I roll my eyes.

Cathy Vitali

Oh, gawd, not her again, sort of thing. We pass it straight up to Mrs Shelper.

Irene Shelper

I'm afraid I had no patience. Some people, in my view, are beyond helping. They will always be dependent. They will always turn to others to solve their problems. I make no apologies for my beliefs that people ought to try to help themselves, at least once in a while.

Tony Carman

When she rang me, I thought, bloody hell, not again! She was a nice girl but not bright. I said to her, listen, love, I can't run the same story again. People will think you're a nutter. If it was a different family with the same story, then we've got something – 'GLC fails again' or something. Same woman with the same problem in two different houses? Give me a break.

'Cabbage' Lacomber

We hadn't spoken to her for months. She sent us a postcard from Southend, we sent something for the lad for his birthday, but you know how it goes – things tail off, don't they? I've been in from work for about half an hour, cup of tea and a Wagon Wheel in front of the telly. Then the phone goes in the hall and the missus answers and I can tell, straightaway, it ain't good tidings. Boots back on. Jacket on. Out the door and off we go, me and the missus, driving over to Perivale. Rush hour, isn't it? Bloody chaos. Missus has got the road atlas on her lap and the A to Z out, sending me all round the bloody houses, but eventually we get there. Donna's on the doorstep, in tears. Front door open, windows open. Not a neighbour in sight but you could tell they were there, behind the net curtains. Donna doesn't want to go inside, says she can't, but she keeps saying, 'Gerard's gone, Gerard's gone.' So the missus takes her to the car. And in goes old muggins. This was a spring evening, almost summer, but that house was like a morgue. There wasn't much furniture and what there was had been smashed to bits or turned over. It was like a whirlwind had been through, know what I mean? I went upstairs – nothing, nobody. Except the hairs on the back of my neck thought otherwise. I looked in the cupboards, under the beds, no sign of the lad. I didn't want to, not much, but I even went up into the loft. Nothing there, either. Then I got out, down the stairs, out the door. And do you know what? The fucking thing slammed itself shut behind me.

Dr Rebecca Roberts
I don't enjoy doing this, you know, but I happen to have checked the Met Office records for that date and, despite it being May, the wind was blowing 30 mile-per-hour gusts in London and the Home Counties. Perhaps Mr Lacomber was too excited to pay much attention to the weather. It is verifiably true, however, that Gerard Kelly disappeared on or about 7 May 1980.

Chris Sitwell, Metropolitan Police
I believe the feeling on the Force was that Donna Kelly was responsible, somehow, or one of her boyfriends. There was no evidence. I'm not sure how hard they looked, mind you.

Sir Francis Cockerell
It did for the G.L.E.A., I think. Too much of quite the wrong kind of publicity. We struggled on for several more years, more as a result of institutional inertia than because of any enthusiasm at the top.

'Cabbage' Lacomber
We lost track of her again. She moved away to Liverpool or somewhere. Couldn't bear it, being in London. I always keep an eye out, though, you know, in case she turns up in the papers, in one of those haunted council house stories. You get a surprising lot of them, you know. A very surprising lot.

Rainbow Pit

When Chris realised that, quite by accident, he had wandered home again after twenty years, he knew he would have to go to the underpass. He had no choice.

Rainbow Pit – that's what the kids had called the space beneath the motorway with its four subway tunnels, sticker-encrusted railings and graffiti-covered, rust-streaked concrete pillars. Years before he ever knew it there had been a mural of a rainbow, a remnant of an aborted community garden. Though the painting was scrubbed away, the name stuck.

He remembered the Pit filled with the sound of scraping skateboards, cider cans being crushed and the thin tap, tap, tap of portable speakers plugged into a knock-off Walkman. Deano and Melon wrestling, scuffed trainers scattering broken glass; Andrew and Dan telling filthy jokes; Nina chewing her nails to nothing and trying not to smile. She didn't want anyone to see the steel of her braces. And overhead, the neverending waterfall roar of north-south traffic.

Now, he recognised it as just the kind of strategic location he'd sought all over the country, from Inverness to Penzance. It was a fairly dry, fairly clean, fairly safe place to set up camp. Nobody used the underpass anymore because there was no reason to do so: they'd knocked down the school, the bus station and the council offices. Now there was just rubble and brambles surrounded by developers' boards advertising luxury apartments, coming soon. There was lots of air, albeit chewy with pollution, and plenty of space – no walls or ceilings with their restraining holds.

This underpass was different, though, because this was where they'd made The Dash. It was where the mental faultline he'd been built upon finally shifted. Rainbow Pit was where he'd last been himself, his old self – the self that slept in beds and smiled and had a sister, brother, mother. It scared him to be there, or was it excitement? The interference and talkback he always heard was more insistent as if trying to convey an important message.

'I don't fucking care, mate,' he said to nobody. 'I ain't fucking bothered.'

It was just an underpass.

He parked his trolley and emptied it so he could turn it on its side as a cage for his head. He made his bed around it: foam roll, sleeping bag and foil blanket. As grey afternoon turned to purple, and sparse orange lights came lazily to life, he ate a meal of white bread and chocolate. Then he climbed into his sleeping bag and put his head into the trolley.

He tried to ignore the voices, images and impulses with which his brain bombarded him when he closed his eyes. The traffic noise helped. It was soothing, shushing him to sleep like mother used to. Rainbow Pit ain't so bad, he thought, as sleep came down.

What woke him, after midnight, was a shrill laugh spinning out across the concrete.

Beyond opening his eyes, Chris didn't move. He had been conditioned over the course of decades to freeze rather than to start at unexpected sounds.

He heard the laugh again. It was a sound he knew – a distinctive high whoop bouncing off the underside of the six-lane road above, double tracked and amplified.

Slowly, Chris turned his head to look through the mesh of the shopping trolley.

Across the central well of the underpass, on the stepped verge, he thought he saw something shift in the shadows.

'Fuck sake, Chris, fuck sake,' he muttered. He closed his eyes and began the incantation he used when reality began to feel especially slippery: 'If you lived in Pigeon Street... Here are the people you could meet... Here are the people who would say... Hello, goodbye, hello...'

The thing about Deano, the thing that set him apart from all the other boys with acne and shaggy hair, was his lack of fear. He had started talking about doing The Dash one spring evening not long before they were due to take their final exams.

'Can you imagine?' he kept saying. 'Can you imagine it, though? It would be fucking immense.'

'Fucking stupid, more like,' said Melon. Chris, Andrew and Dan agreed.

'Yeah, don't be stupid,' said Nina.

The boys, obsessively but unconsciously aware of every non-verbal signal Nina sent, felt a shift in the air. She didn't think The Dash was a good idea, obviously not, but the thought of it brought a flush to her cheeks.

Chris opened his eyes.

Yes, there was definitely somebody there, moving through the darkness, skirting the edge of the light cast from the road above. It was just a person, though – a normal, unknown, potentially murderous person.

Chris had been through this a thousand times. They were usually more scared of him than he was of them. They came near enough to see his form among the tangled bedclothes and heaped possessions before veering away, as afraid of finding a corpse as they were of him attacking. Sometimes, they shouted. Sometimes, they got close enough to piss on him, or lash out with a boot. Once, there was lighter fluid and a flicked match that blew itself out as it spun, by which time the teenager who'd thrown it had gone.

Whoever this was, now, Chris could handle it. Even if, yes, even if he could see now that there were two of them. The laugh, again – Deano's laugh.

The problem with the idea of The Dash was that it was addictive and became a shared fantasy.

'Can you imagine, though?' said Deano. 'We'd be legends.'

'People will want our autographs,' said Andrew, his blue eyes gleaming behind the smudged lenses of his glasses.

'Shame you're all such fucking pussies,' said Melon, turning it into a dare.

Working out how it could be done was half the fun. Between them, they came up with a dozen plans. Dan's idea to do it at three in the morning when, statistically speaking, the motorway would be at its quietest, was dismissed all round as cheating. Melon suggested wearing hi-vis jackets for which there was some cautious approval until Nina frowned and said, 'It's lame,' after which it was never mentioned again.

It was Chris who upped the stakes by suggesting a race. They would all go together, on the count of three, with the winner crowned king.

In his sleeping bag, Chris grasped for the pen knife he kept in his pocket. For several minutes, even though he could tell they were taking steps, the two strangers hadn't seemed to get any closer. Now, suddenly, as if the film had skipped, they were almost upon him. He couldn't see them clearly, not only because his head was on its side, or because of the sliced and noisy light, but because they wore hooded tops which drowned their faces in shadow. Then he saw the tell-tale glint of a smile held together with metal tracks.

The Dash was a disaster. They only did it because they were post-exam, summer holiday drunk, but being drunk made it much worse. They were hesitant, their coordination was bad, they stumbled over their own unfamiliar limbs.

'Get ready,' Deano yelled, watching the oncoming cars, waiting for something like a gap.

'Get set...'

There was no gap, or not as much as Deano thought.

'Go!'

Melon went a moment early and made it across all six lanes – bodily, at least – before his legs folded beneath him. Cars whomped as they passed, kicking grit and pearls of headlight glass into the air. Melon crawled onto the scarce kerb and curled into a quivering hump.

Andrew got clipped by a Ford Fiesta and rolled into the hard shoulder with a broken leg and broken arm, his face scraping across the surface of the road.

Dan made it to the central reservation where, quaking, he crouched by the crash barrier as horns dopplered around him.

Deano tripped and fell flat in the path of an Eddie Stobart that dragged him, instantly lifeless, halfway to the next junction.

Nina saw this happen and, panicking, stopped to cry out. She bounced off the windshield of a Range Rover and was thrown back against the concrete wall that overlooked Rainbow Pit, comprehensively broken.

Chris never moved at all. He just stood there on the start line, pissing himself and crying as sirens came near.

The two figures standing over Chris in the darkness weren't broken, bruised or bloodied. Their faces, the high contours of which he could now see picked out in orange and blue, were perfect – no acne, no picked-at scabs, no adolescent shine. They looked serious. Angry.

As he listened to the white noise from the road above, Chris knew what they wanted.

Struggling to his feet, he smoothed his filthy beard, cleared his throat and spat.

They followed him, at a distance, as he shuffled to the barrier and climbed over onto the road. Broken shoes flapping, he followed the curve, hugging the wall, onto the slip road. Up and up he went, the two shadows at his tail, passed by one car, two cars, a van, another car.

On the hard shoulder, he took his position. Nina fell in on his left, Deano to his right.

Chris looked at the blackness where Deano's face must be, beneath the hood.

'Get ready,' said Chris.

A supermarket delivery lorry threw up a haze of rain and oil.

'Get set.'

Car, car, van, car, car...

'Go.'

Alice Li is Snowed Under

The newspapers had promised 'apocalyptic snow' but Alice Li ignored them. They were always predicting blizzards and gales when the sky delivered only drizzle and damp breeze. But as the afternoon wore on she was forced to concede that, this time, they were right. The flakes fell in sheets and driving became impossible.

'...being advised to stay indoors and only travel if essential...' said a voice on the radio.

She wasn't going to make Manchester, not today. Even if she could get there, the Mayor's office would be shut and the meetings she had scheduled would certainly be cancelled. When she saw a lorry that had skidded into the verge, its trailer tipped, surrounded by blue lights and high-visibility jackets, she decided there was no other choice but to find a hotel.

Of course Amber wouldn't be happy, even though it was she who had told Alice not to cancel the trip, pointing to the swimlane chart and the scheduled deliverables. 'There are too many dependencies,' she'd said. 'Or do you want to tell Stephen that he'll have to tell the Minister that we're going to have to cancel the announcement in February?' Alice certainly didn't want to do that. It would be severely career limiting, as Amber liked to put it. Alice hadn't worked flat out, from school to college to university to Fast Stream without a pause, only to let the weather get in the way.

The next junction was for Wolverhampton. Alice came off the motorway, struggling up the off-ramp in low gear, wheels slipping in the thickening snow. After following a curl of two-lane road smeared with grey sludge, Alice saw the neon light of the Sleeping Beauty Motel – a concrete slab standing proud in a whited-out car park. She pulled in and crawled across the blank space, windscreen wipers scooping gobs of snow back and forth, and parked as close to the front door as possible.

She turned off the engine and the radio faded away. She breathed out with relief, uncomfortably aware of the pumping of her heart.

Fortunately, she'd brought an overnight bag with a change of blouse, socks and underwear, because local authority types sometimes changed the times of meetings at the last minute. She took the bag from the passenger seat, along with her quilted coat, and stepped out into the blizzard.

The gale fluttered and snapped across the empty retail park, hurling snow around and over her. It whooped in her ears and instantly petrified her hands, lips and cheeks. The few steps to the concrete canopy felt like half a mile.

She rushed through the automatic doors and into the warm yellow of the hotel reception. Her body convulsed with shivering as the doors snapped shut and silence fell, except for the royalty-free ambient music drifting, bassless, from hidden speakers. Everything was beige. 'We regret that our restaurant is closed due to staff shortages' read a sign on a metal stand in front of a darkened dining hall.

There was nobody at the desk.

Alice stood on the spot and waited. She sighed. The space was blandly peaceful and, for a moment at least, there was nothing she could or should be doing. Then she frowned: except, of course, she ought to call Amber to confess, and call Manchester to let them know, and call Sue in central services to authorise the payment for a hotel not on the approved supplier's list and…

A movement in her peripheral vision caused her to spin to the left, towards the lifts. There was nobody there but she thought she caught a glimpse of a sliding shadow reflected in the polished steel of the lift doors.

'Good afternoon.'

Alice started at the sudden sound of a voice from her right, at the reception desk.

'Do you have a reservation with us today?'

He was a tall, lean young man with very black skin and a name badge that read EMMANUEL next to English and Italian flags. He wasn't smiling and before she could answer, he spoke again with a mournful note in his voice.

'Terrible weather, innit? I can't go home tonight. I gotta stay here.'

Alice smiled tightly, humping the bag back onto her shoulder.

'I had to come off the motorway,' she said. 'It was getting dangerous out there.'

Emmanuel waited, staring, then repeated his question: 'Do you have a reservation?'

'Oh, uh, no. I'd like a single room for one night, please, if that's at all possible,' she said.

This prompted Emmanuel to move to the next section of the script. He took her name, address, asked to see ID, and took credit card details. He then made a keycard for room 804, sliding it across the counter.

'Top floor, good view, very quiet.'

'Many guests today?'

Emmanuel shook his head like a doctor sharing bad news about a terminal patient.

'Almost nobody.'

She took the lift up eight floors. Synthesised jazz-funk played. She stepped out onto a long corridor lined with doors. There was a window at the far end, plastered with snow and glowing white. She found her room easily enough and let herself in, dumping the bag on the bed.

The room smelled of cigarettes, despite the signs forbidding smoking, and everything was scuffed, chipped or discoloured. The bed was soft, though, and the duvet heavy. There were thick white towels, a desk, a kettle and a TV. She didn't need much else. She even had a couple of packets of instant ramen and a plastic bowl in her emergency overnight bag so she wouldn't need to order room service.

Emmanuel had no doubt oversold the view but there was no way to be sure. All she could see from the window was a shifting, warping wall of white. If she peered hard, she thought she could just discern the edge of the car park as a thumb-smear of pale grey across the canvas. She watched a figure move through the blizzard and was struck by how little this person seemed to be hampered by the wind or cold. A dark, dogged speck almost gliding towards the hotel.

Her phone rang. Rushing to her bag, fumbling, fingers still numb, she answered. It was Amber.

'How are you, Alice? Safe, I hope? I've been watching the news.'

'Yes, thank you. I didn't make it to Manchester, I'm afraid. I've had to pull off the M6 and find a hotel.'

'Oh, right – what a shame.'

Amber was clever. She never said or wrote anything that could possibly sting her during an union intervention or employment tribunal. Alice had worked with her long enough, however, to tell that she was furious.

'I don't want to add to your burden when you're no doubt already feeling at least a little stressed–' She gave her dusty, mummified laugh.

'Oh, no, I'm fine, but–'

'– with end-user outcomes in mind, it would be good if you could arrange a video conference or phone call so we can get this squared away on schedule.'

'I'll see what I can do,' said Alice.

Amber left a silence just long enough to let Alice know how disappointed she was with this weak response and then said: 'Great, thanks, do keep me in the loop.'

Alice called Sue who tried to convince Alice to drive to another hotel five miles away, because it was on the Department's approved list. Alice explained that it was impossible and Sue said: 'Fine, right, so, um, if you could just put that in writing, for the record...' To cover your arse, thought Alice, but agreed to do as Sue had asked.

She set up her laptop on the scratched desk and then realised there was no wi-fi in the hotel. She checked her phone. She had no data connection there, either, perhaps because of the storm. No video-conference with Manchester, then, and no emails to Sue or anyone else. It was only two o'clock and she ought to do some kind of work, but what? There was a paper for the board due. Perhaps she could work on that, offline.

She glanced at the bed. The drive had been exhausting and it couldn't hurt to sit for two minutes. Then, once she'd sat down, she couldn't resist the temptation to lie down – just for a moment. Kicking off her low-heeled shoes, she reclined and knitted her fingers over her belly. It was a long time since she'd found herself anywhere near a bed during the day. Even at weekends, she usually ended up working, or worrying about work, with no time for naps. But there, in the muffled gale and the soft blue snow light, she released a thirty-year-long sigh.

Arms flinging out in terror, a numb-tongued shout into complete darkness.

'Who's there?'

Alice thrashed until she woke herself up. She rubbed gum from her eyes and saliva from her cheek. She remembered where she was and groaned. She held a hand to her aching head. Did she have Paracetamol in her bag? Or maybe some water would do the job.

She listened to the room for a moment. It seemed to hold the echo of a sound, the scent of someone recently departed. She would have to remember to double lock the door and maybe put a chair in front of it.

The window was yellow, now – fluorescent retail park lighting diffused by snow emulsified in the swirling air. Alice lowered her feet to the floor and stumbled stiffly to the bathroom. She couldn't find the light switch at first and then, when she did, it didn't seem to work, so she drank lukewarm water from the tap, feeling her way with her fingers.

She hoped Amber hadn't called while she was sleeping. She wondered if she ought to work now, until late, to make up the time.

There was a knock at the door.

What was this? Emmanuel, perhaps, coming to tell her the hotel was closing? Or bringing an extra blanket, maybe – the room did feel cold.

She peered through the peephole. The fish-eye showed an empty corridor – though only just vacated, Alice knew, somehow. An oddly familiar sweet tobacco tang brushed at the edge of her senses. She sniffed but couldn't catch it again.

Alice snapped the door open and stepped out. Left, nothing, but to the right, disappearing around the corner, the last glimpse of a shape in black.

'Hello? Did you knock on my door?' Alice called into the empty hall. There was no reply. 'Did you… did you want something? Hello?'

Breaking into an ungainly half-jog, she made it to the corner but all she found was a hundred metres of mottled carpet, thirty brown doors and the green glow of a fire exit sign.

The next morning, she could hear the silence of the snow. It had stopped falling but not before covering her car, the car park, and most of the details of the landscape for miles around. She checked her phone and found it had no connection at all.

'Morning, madam,' said a weary Emmanuel when she went down for breakfast. 'I'm so sorry to say that we are snowed in completely.'

She glanced towards the sliding doors. They had been locked off and presented a wall of grey-blue. There was a slit of sunlight at the top.

'There are very much worse places to be, however,' said Emmanuel. 'Plenty of food, good emergency generator if, God forbid it, the electricity lines come down, and of course more than fifty TV channels.'

'Got any books?'

Emmanuel gave a nod-shake-bow.

'Oh, yes, plenty of books. People leave them behind. I will bring out a box for you to take your pick after breakfast.'

He gestured towards the dining room and Alice followed the line indicated by his long fingers.

The dining room was as big as a school hall and the five other guests had arranged themselves, as British people always will, so as to leave the maximum possible space between themselves.

A man with a bald brown head and a wrinkled shirt; a muscular builder with a slogan in Polish on his T-shirt and paint-spattered boots; a miserable middle-aged couple staring at their phones; and, finally, what looked like an old lady dressed in black – a hump of dark, dusty cotton, a curl of grey hair. She was in a corner facing the wall, pouring green tea from an iron pot into a dainty cup with no handles.

Alice looked for a seat. The necessary distancing calculations ran in her head and she deposited her key on a table away from the window, near the toasters, and went to fetch coffee and juice.

A radio murmured. '...since the winter of 1963, according to the Met Office. Further snowfall is expected later today with storms clearing by midnight, leaving a bright, clear day across the country from tomorrow morning. Now, let's see if these lads can get those motorways moving – it's Mike and the Mechanics.'

Emmanuel came through the dining room stopping at each occupied table – one, two, three, four, then Alice.

'No cooked breakfast today, I'm afraid – no cooks! But we have toast, pastries, cereals and if you like, I can boil an egg.' He gritted his yellow teeth in a tense smile and she knew that having to boil an egg would make him very unhappy, so she shook her head.

'Toast is fine.'

As he began to move away, she grabbed at his sleeve.

He stopped, looked panicked, and rubbed his arm where the fabric had been pinched.

'Yes, madam?'

'Can I have a pot of green tea?'

Emmanuel shook his head and stuck out his bottom lip.

'We don't have green tea, sorry – only summer berry, fresh peppermint, soothing camomile and traditional English breakfast.'

He drifted away.

Alice, irritated, looked towards the old woman's table. She was gone and the table was clear. There was no teapot, no teacup, no sign that she had ever existed.

After breakfast, Alice looked through the box of paperbacks in reception for something to read once the board paper was drafted – the only piece of work she could do. She actually wanted to read a thriller but a voice in her head tutted at her, told her it would be a waste of precious time, so she took a copy of *Bleak House* instead.

Throughout the whole of the day, she didn't read a single page. She didn't write anything worthwhile, either, only moving around the words she'd already produced for the executive summary. At first, she reproached herself for her idleness, until logic won out: what could she do? Nothing. It wasn't her fault. So, slowly, she began to think about starting to consider the vague possibility of relaxing.

She watched the window turn from white to blue to orange. She ate a limp room service pizza that Emmanuel microwaved. Finally, she did something she hadn't done since she was a little girl: she turned on the TV and watched nothing in particular, for hours, until she began to drowse.

She didn't sleep that night, not exactly. Hotel rooms are never really dark, even with the lights off and curtains drawn, because there's always a glow leaking from somewhere – under the door, the air-conditioning control panel, the gap at the top of the curtains – so she lay in the almost-blackness, at turns fretting and fantasising.

After a series of short, disturbing nightmares, none of which she could quite remember even though they left her heart knocking, she got up to check the time. Three thirty three.

Then a memory came, or a memory of a dream: the veined hands of an old woman setting and then winding a bedside alarm clock – one of those clamshell clocks designed for travel.

'Three-thirty three, all the threes, very lucky,' Alice muttered to herself. She frowned. She didn't believe in any of that stuff. Neither did her parents.

She got up and walked, stretching and yawning, to the window. Pulling back the curtain, she looked over the car park.

The snow had stopped and the air was clear so that distant lights picked out hillsides and suburbs.

Squinting, she peered at the off-white sheet through which a stripe had been ploughed, right up the front door of the hotel.

There was somebody down there, waiting, in the middle of the channel in the snow.

A black shape, small and crooked – a figure that, for the first time, she recognised without doubt.

Alice let the curtain fall back and stood in the almost-darkness listening to the hum of the heating and her own short, fast breaths.

She dressed quickly, pulling on her quilted coat and unsuitable shoes, and slipped out of the room, letting the door close with a whisper of insulation on wood.

The corridor was cold and smelled stale. The lights were on but flickered sickly in her periphery. She took the stairs, not the lift, and entered reception through a fire door beside a set of vending machines. The sliding doors had been cleared of snow, now, and had become murky mirrors with the night behind them. She punched a green button and, after a moment, the doors opened.

She stepped into the cold. Her breath condensed, creating a wavering veil that came and went. Brown grit ground beneath her feet as she stepped slowly, reluctantly, towards the old woman.

Yes, it was definitely her. She was wearing the clothes she always had one when she visited or when they went out for dinner – a two-piece suit with thick seams, as stiff as cardboard. The polished black handbag gleamed. Her tights sagged around her bony knees. The black pumps she always wore pointed inward.

Alice didn't want to look at her face. She was afraid it would be decayed or distorted. As she came within a few steps, she felt her eyes being pulled upward. Her heart thumped. The face was perfect, exactly as it had been when Alice last saw it twenty-five years before. The eyes weren't filmed or fogged but wet and glowing. She looked at Alice with a severe expression, expectant.

The air seemed heavy with potential and sweet with perfume – Yardley English Lavender mixed with a background note of cloves.

Alice wondered what she was supposed to do. Then she heard her own voice, dead against the surrounding snow.

'Are you proud of me, Grandma?'

She didn't know what had made her ask that question but she knew the answer was important.

Grandma's face opened in a smile as warm as midday sun.

'Of course I am.'

The electricity intensified, the perfume bloomed, and somehow Alice Li both passed out and woke up at the same moment.

Afterword: Council houses – haunted by something

In Britain, hauntings occur in ancient manor houses, old inns, and Gothic asylums – places whose very age makes them groan and creak, where shadows sit deep, and which are scarred by the lingering imprint of lives lived and lost.

And yet what is arguably the most famous British ghost story of the 20th century took place somewhere quite different – in a humble council house, only half a century old, in Enfield, north London.

There, between 1977 and 1979, sisters Margaret and Janet Hodgson were the centre of a poltergeist manifestation that has inspired books, articles, multiple TV dramas and even a recent Hollywood film. But the Enfield Poltergeist – I think it deserves the capital letters – is far from being the only such story and was certainly not the first.

'The world of the ghost is riddled with class,' wrote Roger Clarke in his 2012 *Natural History of Ghosts*, 'and the poltergeist is occasionally tagged as "the council house ghost".' Here are just a few examples of the council house ghost in the wild.

Weedon, Northamptonshire, 1947-50
In 1950 the tenants of a red-brick council house on Queen Street, built only in 1945-46, reported having seen a figure glide through the hall and then disappear. Mrs Thomas Bicknell (her own name is not given) first saw the ghost in around 1947, as reported in the *Northampton Mercury and Herald* for 6 January 1950:

> *She and her late husband, Mr Thomas Bicknell – a man with 23 years' service in the Royal Artillery and*

> *not given to imagining things – had just finished a game of cards when they heard a rustling and tapping noise coming from the direction of the hall... Their dog, a large Airedale retriever, rose to its feet, raised its hackles and growled... Mr Bicknell went into the hall but could see nothing. The dog went up the stairs, still growling, and his master followed. Again there was nothing, but as he turned to descend the stairs, he saw a ghostly figure glide through the hall, go into the kitchen, and disappear. Mrs Bicknell, sitting in the living room, saw it too.*

After her husband died, Mrs Bicknell saw the ghost a second time, on Christmas Eve 1949, doing the same gliding and disappearing act. When her distress story was reported at a council meeting it was met with laughter. 'This added amenity warrants an increase in the rent,' said Mr D.H. Jelley, following in the grand gentlemanly tradition of scoffing at superstitious peasants.

Earby, Lancashire, 1954

Mr E. Peasey, a chimney sweep, evacuated his wife and nine children to a single downstairs room in their council house at 1 Melrose Street as a result of 'queer things' happening elsewhere in the house, and multiple ghostly apparitions. Here's a summary from the *Burnley Express and News* for 16 October that year:

> *[For] three years, doors had opened on their own, footsteps had been heard overhead, crockery had flown into the air and pictures had gone crooked... One of the boys, 14-year-old [Bobby] described a shadow in his bedroom. At first he thought it was a reflection but*

> *it advanced to the middle of his room and then began to tickle his feet and scratch him... The 'thing' was white, with no arms or legs, and when an alarm clock went off it had backed into the corner and disappeared... Ten-year-old Kathleen described seeing two hooded figures 'floating' and similar shapes were described by others in the family.*

Another report, from the *Barnoldswick and Earby Times* for 15 October, adds more details: a bright light seen in an upstairs room, door knobs turning on their own, and two of the children waking their father to report that they had 'seen a man in Daddy's attic'. A small twist: this was apparently an older slum property with gaslighting rather than a modern council property and the story came to light precisely because Mr Peasey wrote to the council requesting a new house.

Sunderland, County Durham/Tyne & Wear, 1957

In March 1957 Norman and Audrey Dixon caused a stir when they reported that the council house in General Havelock Road, Sunderland, into which they had recently moved with their three young children was haunted in a rather colourful fashion, as recounted in the *Birmingham Post* for 23 October 1957:

> *[The ghost] takes the form of a zig-zag line [which] appears on the wall of their living room.... 'The first night they slept upstairs, sheets were ripped off the bed and fingers dug into their chests...', Mr Dixon said. 'A few nights later I felt something clammy on my back and so did my wife. There seemed to be no air in the room. We staggered downstairs and took the family to my brother's house.'*

This case was taken seriously enough by the local vicar that he appealed to the Bishop of Jarrow, J.A. Ramsbotham, who visited the property and conducted a ten-minute blessing service on 22 March, including the sprinkling of holy water. But when journalist Ken Culley followed up ('I was guest in the haunted house', *Newcastle Evening Chronicle*, 25/03/1957) the Dixons told him that the exorcism had been effective for only 24 hours and that the 'unwanted visitor' had returned in full force. They too were eventually evicted after refusing to pay their rent in protest at the Council's refusal to let them move to another house (*Newcastle Journal*, 29/10/1957). Another family, the Rowes, moved into the house in November 1957 and reportedly found it 'all quiet' (*Newcastle Evening Chronicle*, 05/11/1957).

South Shields, Tyneside, 1965

It was in the bedroom of a house on Thames Lane that Edna Wahab, her mother-in-law Lilian Seff and sister-in-law Saidah Seff, saw the ghost of a nun in February 1965. One journalist, James Stokoe, got permission from the family, who were Muslims from the city's Yemeni community, to bring a dog into the house. Though Stokoe himself saw nothing, the dog's hackles rose and, barking, it refused to enter the bedroom (*Newcastle Journal*, 08/02/1965). The house was exorcised by a 'healer', to Mrs Wahab's satisfaction, on the night of 8 February that year (*Newcastle Evening Chronicle*, 09/02/1965).

Plymouth, Devon, 1966

Mr and Mrs Stanley Robertson lived in a first-floor council flat at 244 Union Street. Their ghost whistled, sobbed, threw their clothes around and moved the furniture. Eric Nuttall, chairman of the city housing committee, dismissed the tenants' complaints: 'If the Robertson family are desperately unhappy, they might prefer to find themselves alternative accommodation.' The Reverend David Vickery, vicar of St Peter's, carried out a service of exorcism on 20 April that year.(*Torbay Express and South Devon Echo*, 21/04/66.)

Swindon, Wiltshire, 1966

A brand new council house in Penhill Drive in Swindon was the subject of national press coverage. Gladys and Robert Tucker, who lived with their adult children Beryl and Victor, asked to be moved after they saw a shadowy figure on the landing and strange lights on the walls (*Daily Mirror*, 04/04/1966). The council sent men round to check the electrics and the lights, but found nothing wrong. Eventually, the council reluctantly agreed to rehouse them. 'The family were in a terrible state and the wife kept crying,' said Arthur Camden, chairman of the Swindon housing committee. Despite his apparent scepticism, the council had the house exorcised by a priest before allocating it to new tenants. In his 1967 book *Swindon: An Awkward Size for a Town*, Kenneth Hudson reported this incident as a blot upon the town's image.

Newton-le-Willows, Lancashire, 1968

In March 1968, Gerald and Audrey Burke, 34 and 31, moved out of their council house on Fern Avenue as a result of 'tappings, loud thumps and the breaking of glass', and the ghost of 'an old lady.... wearing a white hat'. Mrs Burke asked the Council to re-house the family (*Aberdeen Evening Express*, 13/03/1968). It seems the Burkes were not the first tenants to complain of such occurrences (*Coventry Evening Telegraph*, 27/02/1968) and the Council, flummoxed, resorted to sending in first a Roman Catholic priest, Father Gerald Walker (*Birmingham Daily Post*, 27/02/1968) and then 'psychic experts' – brothers Alan and James Bell, from Formby – to exorcise the property. The Bells were convinced by the evidence and urged the council to move the Burke family, even offering to rent the house themselves while they continued their investigations (*Coventry Evening Telegraph*, 04/03/1968). I haven't been able to pin down what happened next but I can say this: Fern Avenue no longer exists, even though Ivy, Pine, Larch, Ash and Laurel avenues do.

Newcastle upon Tyne, 1972

The Calvert family home on Whitehouse Road had good reason to be haunted: it was the former home of Mary Bell, who murdered two children when she was herself only 10 years old. According to a report in the *Sunday Mirror* (28/05/1972) the Calverts claimed to hear the sound of a baby crying. Windows spontaneously shattered. Doors swung open by themselves. And gas taps turned themselves on while the family slept. The Calverts asked to be moved, of course.

Coventry, West Midlands, 1973

In 1973 it was a council house in Stoke Heath that scared away its residents. Lynne and John Edwards moved their family into a single room at 63 Hill Side for mutual protection after they heard 'whining noises and footsteps', and felt the house turn freezing cold in an instant. An exorcism was held but, Edwards said, 'It has been worse since then.' The family fled in the end, leaving all their furniture. (*Coventry Evening Telegraph*, 19/11/1973).

Reading, Berkshire, 1979-80

In the winter of 1979, Noel Kelliher and his wife reported 'bumpings and scrapings in the night followed by an eerie draught and a strong smell of rotten eggs' in their basement flat at number 11 Zinzan Street. Mr Kelliher, a 27-year-old Irish

Catholic, was convinced it was the ghost of Joseph Nee, a neighbour who drowned in the Kennet after swimming while drunk. 'On the night after I identified the body,' said Mr Kelliher, 'we heard thumps and scrapings on the floor of the upstairs front room... We went up and opened the door. There was nothing there, but it was like walking into a freezer... Then I saw this image starting to form just inside the window. It was shaped like a face shrouded in what looked like white cotton wool.' The house was blessed by a priest and the Kellihers were rehoused (*Reading Evening Post*, 16/02/1979).

Then, in the following year, Shirley Du-Val and her husband, Stephen, fled the same council property, demanding to be moved. She said she heard a voice whispering her name over and over again when she was alone in the house. Doors were said to open and close and ornaments were knocked over. Mrs Du-Val worried that a spirit might possess her baby son, Kevin. In this case, the council were more definite in their scepticism: the house was on a main road, they pointed out, and was old. The walls were thin. And the whispering voice? A powerful fridge in the flat next door (*Reading Evening Post*, 13/09/1980).

★ ★ ★

The council house is not such an unusual setting in which to encounter a ghost after all. They are positively prone to it. What can possibly cause these relatively history-less houses, designed to be light and airy, to be such fertile ground for the uncanny?

In America the answer would be an 'Indian burial ground', as in Tobe Hooper's 1982 film *Poltergeist*. But there's no such obvious plot engine – no orphanage or battle site – in any of the cases mentioned above.

It doesn't take much age at all for a house to gain the potential for a haunting. In the 1968 haunting of another

Coventry council house, this time at Treherne Road, the anxious 37-year-old resident, Miss Barbara Mills, connected a serious of spontaneous fires with rumours she had heard of a wartime suicide at the property (*Birmingham Daily Post*, 22/10/1968). And the Dixons in Sunderland invited a local psychic, James Long, to conduct a séance at the General Havelock Road house which resulted in a message from a drowned man, John McKenzie, who apologised for the trouble he had caused, but mentioned that there was also the "earthbound spirit of a woman" (*Newcastle Journal*, 29/04/1957).

In more concrete terms (no pun intended) is there perhaps something about the way the houses were constructed? In the Sunderland case, journalist Ken Culley slept in the haunted bedroom but, despite apparently making every effort to spook himself, saw no evidence of anything supernatural. What he did observe was that the design of the house made it simultaneously cold and stuffy. Opening the window, he said, caused a localised breeze to swirl around the foot of the bed, numbing his feet. Light and airy may have been the intention but large rooms with high ceilings, sparsely furnished, offer great potential for echoes, reflections and strange circulations.

Then there is the question of location, at which I'll indulge my own memories of growing up on an estate. Council developments often occupy what in the jargon of psychogeography are called 'edgelands', neither town nor country. They can resemble lonesome frontier towns, looking out over fields or wasteland. All that space, a joy on a summer afternoon, has its flipside: winds whistling across shopping precincts and playing fields, or along showpiece boulevards. Long, dark gardens with no walls and too many shadows. Neighbours who are strangers and temporary. And family members far away, on other estates or in other towns.

Council houses – haunted by something

A bedroom for the parents and one for each child sounds like the ideal unless you're used to something more intimate and find yourself alone in the small hours listening to silence, staring at a strange shape moving across an excess of freshly-plastered wall.

With that in mind, it's perhaps unsurprising that many of the cases described above resulted in the afflicted families bunking up together in a single room, or crashing with neighbours or family. A kind of stress reaction to being cleared from the intimacy of the slums?

Roger Clarke's point about class is a good one, too. He suggests that, at least until recently, middle class people were less likely to *publicly* report experiences of ghosts, even if they might admit to them privately. Talk of ghosts is viewed as evidence of either peasant stupidity, or working class mendacity, and either way 'showing off' by talking about this kind of thing for whatever reason is 'common'.

Finally, there is the very fact of the stress of life on an estate. I should be clear here that, in my experience, English council estates aren't as bad as some people like to suggest; but nor are they, in practice, anything like Utopian. There is crime and there is anti-social behaviour. One example: our back door-knob used to rattle after dark when my Dad worked nights. A small thing, but stress inducing. My Mum got into the habit of having my Uncle's Army riot baton by her armchair or next to the bed, and I got out of the habit of sleeping soundly, just in case intruders needed seeing off. Living like that, never quite relaxed, wears you down and sets you on edge.

Then there is poverty itself, which might mean a lack of food, or of heating, and which itself chews at one's sanity and sense of self.

I cannot stand it much longer…. I am living on my nerves', wrote Peasey, the Earby chimney sweep with nine children to feed, in his letter to the council. He was certainly haunted by something, ghosts or otherwise.

Printed in Great Britain
by Amazon